PEARLY AND PIG

AND THE
GREAT HAIRY BEAST

SUE WHITING

WALKER BOOKS

First published in Great Britain 2022 by Walker Books Ltd
87 Vauxhall Walk, London SE11 5HJ

2 4 6 8 10 9 7 5 3 1

Text © 2022 Sue Whiting
Illustrations © 2022 Rebecca Crane

The right of Sue Whiting and Rebecca Crane to be identified as author and
illustrator respectively of this work has been asserted in accordance with the
Copyright, Design and Patents Act 1988

Printed and bound in Great Britain by Clays Ltd

All rights reserved. No part of this work may be reproduced,
transmitted or stored in an information retrieval system in any form
or by any means, graphic, electronic or mechanical, including
photocopying, taping and recording, without prior written
permission from the publisher.

British Library Cataloguing in Publication Data:
a catalogue record for this book is available from the British Library

ISBN 978-1-5295-0449-1

www.walker.co.uk

FOR LIZZIE –

thank you for being so fearless
and creative during our imaginary
expeditions to Antarctica. I couldn't
have written this book without you.

CHAPTER 1

It was the wall-mounted Adventure Phone's non-stop mooing that made Pearly Woe do it.

She knew she shouldn't.

And she had tried her best not to.

She had even fled to the attic. But three rickety floors up, wedged between dusty trunks and teetering piles of junk, she still couldn't escape it. The phone's mooing was impossible to ignore.

And Pig wasn't helping. Not one bit. He had been squealing for over an hour now, his snout waving back and forth like windscreen wipers in a rainstorm, his pink eyes frantic as he paced in front of the phone, oinking, OINKY OINKY NO-NO! OINKY OINKY NO-NO!, which was Pig for *TROUBLE, I SMELL TROUBLE.*

But still the phone MOOED and MOOED and MOOED. So Pearly had traipsed back downstairs, checking her mobile phone yet again.

Still no coverage.

Still no messages.

"Dove diavolo sei?" Where on earth are you? Pearly pleaded in Italian, which was her go-to language when she was stressed.

And boy, was she stressed. Her parents had gone to Lemon Tree Village shops to get some milk and bread. It should have taken them less than an hour.

It had been three.

Sure, the heavens were chucking down rain like there was no tomorrow. Sure, the wind was bending the pines so they almost touched the ground. But three hours to get bread and milk? That was unheard of.

Maybe they've been swept off the road and into the swirling currents of the Lemon Tree River? Pearly worried. *Maybe they've been in a head-on crash with a semi-trailer laden with steel girders, or live sheep – or both! Maybe they've taken a wrong turn and ended up in the African Animal Safari Theme Park and are surrounded by a mob of angry elephants...*

MOO! MOO! That phone. It wouldn't stop.

Pearly stood before it, her hand poised, her teeth feasting on her bottom lip.

OINKITY! oinked Pig, which was pig for, *NO!*

"But it won't stop," wailed Pearly, before launching into her best piggy cursing. "Smoky bacon and pork chops! Leg ham and apple sauce!"

OINKITY! warned Pig again as a gust of wind lashed rain against the windows.

The glass rattled. The shutters flapped. Outside, something thumped to the ground. Woe Mansion felt as if it was being torn from its clifftop perch above the Lemon Tree River, as if its very foundations were bravely clinging to the rocky ground for dear life, and it would only take one particularly fierce gust to send the whole house hurtling into the sky. Pearly reached for the phone, fingers trembling.

OINKITY!

Pig was right. She shouldn't answer it – she knew that. The Adventure Phone was a secret landline for members of the Adventurologists' Guild. No one else had the number. Only Guild members were allowed to answer it.

Pearly was not a member. Not yet, anyhow.

But what if there's an emergency? Pearly fretted. *What if there's an approaching tsunami or a category five hurricane or a one-hundred-year flood surging down the river?*

Pearly wrung her hands. What to do?

MOO! MOO! Why wouldn't it stop?

OINKY OINKY NO-NO! Pig paced and squealed. *TROUBLE, I SMELL TROUBLE.*

The Adventure Phone never rang and rang like this. But then, her parents or Grandpa Woe were always around to answer it. Maybe that was it!

Maybe it was her parents using the Adventure Phone because the mobile network was down. Maybe they needed her help. But why would they ring her for help? She was the last person they would call. In terms of who to rely on in an emergency, she was definitely not their go-to girl.

Maybe ... maybe it was a TEST!

That was it. Her father loved setting tests.

Pearly had been training as an Adventurologist since the day she turned eight years old. And ever since that day, her father had been setting her tests. It was almost a hobby for him.

She could pass the test. She could!

She was far from being fully trained, and not exactly the most promising student, but surely she knew something that would help in a situation like this.

She racked her brain for inspiration.

If it *was* her father setting a test, then it would probably be something from *Rules and Guidelines for Young Adventurologists*, or the *RAG*, as everyone in the Guild called it. Ricky Woe was a stickler for rules and the *RAG* was like a bible to him. Pearly raced into the library and grabbed the book from her study table. It was well worn, the corners curling, the pages splattered with splotches of hot chocolate and smudges of Vegemite and tomato sauce. She hastily opened to the page listing the rules.

Rule 1: Stay alive.

Of course.

Rule 2: Do not take or destroy.

Irrelevant!

Rule 3: Tread lightly.

Not helpful!

Rule 4: Do not disturb the balance.

As if.

Rule 5: Never answer the Adventure Phone – unless an authorized member of the Adventurologists' Guild.

Dang.

She gave up on the rules and thumbed through to the "Guidelines for Surviving Sticky Situations" chapter. Surely this would count as a sticky situation. Wouldn't it?

She slid her finger down the page, searching for something useful.

1. Take initiative...
2. Think outside the box...
3. Keep your eyes and ears open and your wits about you...

Mamma mia! Pearly slammed the book shut. This was not helping at all!

MOO! MOO! MOO!

That was it. She couldn't stand it any more.

"*Basta!*" Enough.

She had to answer it.

She must.

She did.

OINKY OINKY NO-NO! squealed Pig. *TROUBLE, I SMELL TROUBLE.*

He was darn right.

CHAPTER 2

"Oh, Pearly! You picked up!" It was her mother, Angel Woe.

Pearly's stomach plummeted. It *was* a test. A test that she had just failed. Another to add to her long list of failures. At this rate she would be 102 before she was a member of the Guild.

"Pearly! Pearly! Are you still there?" Angel persisted.

Pearly contemplated hanging up and pretending that she hadn't answered, but it wasn't in her nature to deceive her mother.

"Yes, Mum, I'm here. I'm sorry. I—"

"Don't be sorry. You did the right thing. We wanted you to answer – that's why we kept ringing. We knew you wouldn't disobey Rule 5 without a reason, so we had our fingers and toes crossed that you would remember to *take initiative*, like it says in "Surviving Sticky Situations". I am proud of you, Pearly."

Pearly was stunned. These were not words she was accustomed to hearing.

"I passed?" stammered Pearly, beaming, as a fierce gust rocked the mansion and rain pounded the windows.

"Passed?" said her mother. "Pass..." Her mother's voice trailed off. There was a commotion in the background. It sounded like some kind of scuffle or argument. Her mother's muffled voice rose above the racket. "Yes, yes. I will. I am! I am. Leave me be." Pearly's pride backflipped into worry.

"Pearly, listen carefully," Angel continued. "We have an important mission for you."

"Mission? For me?" Anxiety churned in Pearly's gut so fiercely she thought she might throw up. *"Mamma mia! Non so se sono pronto per... Mamma—"*

"Speak English, Pearly," Angel interrupted. "This is serious."

"Sorry, Mum... but I don't know if I'm ready for—"

"You're ready. You have to be. *We need you, Pearly.*" There was a desperation in her mother's words that sent chills racing along Pearly's arms. In the background she could hear a female voice she didn't recognize shout, "Hurry up!"

Pearly gulped and pressed speaker, so Pig could hear too.

"Pearly, we need you to get our polar gear and adventure packs – Little Piggy's also. They're all in

14

the shed at the back of the barn. The big barn by the water's edge."

Pig started turning in circles, the hairs on the top of his head bristling. OINKY OINKY NO-NO, he whimpered.

Pearly was confused. What was her mother going on about? No one ever called Pig *Little Piggy* – that nursery rhyme gave him nightmares. *This little piggy went to market...* Everyone knew what that meant. Pork chops and bacon, that's what. And they didn't *have* a barn, let alone a *big* barn by the water's edge with a *shed*. All their gear was kept in the basement carved into the cliff beneath the house. Was her mother ill? Was she having a brain bleed? Had she been drugged? Worries crowded into Pearly's mind.

"What barn—" she tried, but her mother didn't let her finish.

"An Emmeline Woods contacted your father before the service outage. She's rather famous – on the telly and in all the magazines – and she'd heard about my missions to locate the Great Hairy Beast of Antarctica. She's a big fan. Of the beast, that is, not me."

"GET ON WITH IT!" That voice in the background again. Angry and loud this time, female with a distinct American twang. *Midwestern America*, thought Pearly.

"Anyhow, she asked us to meet her at Port Clementine. So we did and now she wants us to go with her to Antarctica – there have been new sightings. Enormous paw prints and eyewitness accounts of a gigantic furry beast. Black and brown stripes. This could be our chance to prove its existence at last." There was excitement in Angel's voice now and that made Pearly relax slightly. *Dieu merci,* she thought in French – her comfort language. *Thank goodness.* This was the mother she knew. The passionate mother who always took fifty words to say what could be said in five.

"She wants Little Piggy." *Mamma mia!* Not this again.

Pig plopped to the floor and hid his head behind his trotters. OINKY OINKY NO-NO, he snivelled.

"She knows about Pig?"

"Yes. She seems to. So bring Little Piggy and all the gear in the dinghy and meet us at the public jetty at Port Clementine as soon as you can. Grandma Woe is on her way to look after you while we're away."

"You mean Grand*pa* Woe..."

"No. Grandma."

"Esmeralda?"

"Don't call her that, Pearly. You know she finds it disrespectful." There was more commotion in the background. Was that her father's voice sounding sharp and frustrated? Ricky Woe was always so cool and calm. What was going on?

16

"Mum, are you all right?"

"Of course I am. Now hurry along with our gear and Little Piggy. And don't worry, Pearly – just remember that Little Piggy's snout never lies."

The phone went dead. Pearly plopped to the floor, the receiver still in her hand. *Don't worry!* That was a tall order.

Especially for Pearly.

Especially when it was obvious that something was not right.

Especially when it was obvious that something was desperately wrong.

Why would her mother call Pig *Little Piggy*? That was too odd for words.

But what she had said about her grandmother was even odder. Esmeralda refused to be called Grandma – she said she was too young and vital to be a granny. And there was no way she could come and look after Pearly. Esmeralda was looking after her ancient father, Wei Wong, in Singapore.

OINKY OINKY NO-NO, Pig wheezed.

"Pig's snout never lies," whispered Pearly. Her parents were in trouble. And Pearly was worried.

Mamma mia! Questo è terribile.

This is terrible.

CHAPTER 3

The little yellow dinghy putted downriver through the lashing rain with a soggy Pearly and miserable Pig on board. The adventure packs and polar gear were stacked under a tarpaulin.

Pearly gripped the tiller tightly, her knuckles turning white with the strain of keeping the boat on course in the wild summer storm. She pushed her wet curls up under her hood and wiped the rain out of her eyes, trying not to worry about what lay ahead. But not worrying was not one of Pearly's strengths, and Angel's anguished words – *Little Piggy's snout never lies* – rang through her head like a fire alarm.

Her mother was definitely warning her – that much Pearly was certain of. But what was Pearly meant to do with that warning? Sweat beaded on her upper lip and nightmarish thoughts swamped her.

The boat hit a wave and bumped up then down heavily, spray washing over the pair of them.

Pearly tightened the hood of her rain jacket and adjusted course to avoid the rocky edge of Lemon Tree Passage. The river was churning, the waters turned muddy from the torrential rain. Jagged sandstone cliffs plunged from low-hanging clouds to the water's edge on either side, squeezing the little dinghy into the narrowest and most treacherous section of the river. It was tricky to navigate in fine weather, but in pelting rain and high wind, and with the surging currents littered with fallen branches and other debris, it was almost impossible. Pearly squinted through the rain, keeping alert.

Keep your eyes and ears open and your wits about you. Pearly recalled the chapter in the *RAG* on "Surviving Sticky Situations" – a topic that was all-important for serious adventurologists-in-the-making. Her mother had thought she had "used initiative" when she answered the phone, when in truth she had just been desperate. But there was no doubt she was in the middle of a Super Sticky Situation right now. A damp one, for sure, but that didn't wash away any of the stickiness, and she needed to use the guidelines for real this time.

Pearly's eyes fell on Pig. He was standing stoically at the front of the boat, rocking and bumping and struggling to stay in one place, his snout held high.

Pearly's heart panged at the sight of him. She only hoped that she wasn't delivering him into some kind of trap. Her mind became crammed with images of the "famous" Emmeline Woods waiting for Pig at the dock, dressed in a butcher's apron and holding an enormous carving knife above her head. Did Emmeline Woods want to take Pig to the meat market, like the nursery rhyme said? Was that what her mother meant? But what did that have to do with the Great Hairy Beast and Antarctica? Even Pearly could recognize that this was her overactive imagination being supremely overactive. Emmeline Woods would hardly be on the telly and in the magazines as a famous butcher. She pushed the picture out of her mind, and tried to think more logically.

The barn. Her mother had mentioned a barn. And a shed.

What could that mean?

She must be thinking about this all wrong.

Think outside the box. That was one of Grandpa Woe's favourites from the *RAG*. It's what he always told Pearly to do when she was trying to solve the challenges and puzzles he set her each morning. He said it would be good practice for when she was a real adventurologist, and that it applied to everyday life as well as sticky situations.

LOG AHEAD, Pig oinked from the bow. Pearly diverted in the nick of time, the log grazing the side of the dinghy as they passed.

Think! she urged herself, trying to channel Grandpa Woe's calm wisdom. *Think outside the box.*

She recalled the rhyming puzzles Grandpa Woe often challenged her with. Maybe that's it. Maybe the clues rhymed with what her mother really meant. She ran through the possibilities in her head.

Barn. *Yarn. Darn. Farm. Harm!*

Yikes.

Shed. *Bed. Fed. Ted. Red. Head. Dread. Dead!*

Dead! Gulp. Pearly put the brakes on that line of thinking.

She had never been good at Grandpa's challenges and puzzles anyhow. Languages were her strength – all twenty-seven of them, including several animal languages. It was an extraordinary ability, kept a deep dark secret by her family.

But what use was it to her now?

None. Zip. Zilch. *Bèn shǒu bèn jiǎo.* (Mandarin.) *Nichts.* (German.) *Ninguno.* (Spanish.) *Oinkity-o.* (Pig.)

Regardless, she had to keep trying. She couldn't let Pig down. His safety was in her hands, even though there was no way she was ready for this. She knew it. Her parents knew it. Even Pig knew it. Adventuring was her passion. But it hadn't been coming naturally to her, and the past few years of training had only proved that.

Pearly sighed and wiped her soggy face.

Pig grunted like a foghorn into the misty air.

Finally, Port Clementine emerged ghost-like through the fog and rain.

A tremble started in Pearly's legs, and Italian phrases came bubbling up within her.

Up ahead, at the end of the public jetty, Pearly could make out three people clad in dark raincoats. Her parents and Emmeline Woods, no doubt.

But as she drew closer, she realized something was wrong. Very wrong.

Angel Woe was tall and athletic – a trait she had inherited from her Icelandic heritage. Ricky Woe was strong and athletic too, but he was much shorter than his wife. So much so that he could fit snugly under her armpit.

This was not the picture that was forming on the jetty.

There was a woman – as expected.

But the woman was bookended by two enormous and mightily bearded giants.

Pearly's parents were nowhere in sight.

CHAPTER 4

"You took your sweet ole time now didn't you, honeybun?" the woman said as Pearly threw the rope to her.

"Are you Emmeline Woods?" Pearly asked.

The woman tossed the rope over the jetty bollard, then pushed her fur-lined hood off her head and gazed at Pearly through ridiculously long eyelashes. "Well, I don't think I'm Santa Claus, honey, and these two are definitely not my Christmas elves. So I guess I must be." Blonde waves of hair framed her face and she cast a dazzling smile at Pearly, showing off the brightest set of ultra-white teeth Pearly had ever seen. "Of course I'm Emmeline Woods. Who else would I be?" she said with a chuckle, as if it was inconceivable that Pearly hadn't recognized her. "But please, call me Ms Woods. OK?"

Pearly wasn't sure what to make of this woman. Was Ms Emmeline Woods some sort of movie star?

Is that why she was famous? Her teeth certainly looked like movie star teeth. And the shiny perfect blonde waves.

"Hurry up now. You're late." Her voice was light, but Pearly was sure she could hear a tiny hint of threat hidden in its twang.

"Where are my parents?" Pearly asked, fear making her tingle.

"Well, with you being so late and all, they had to board and get themselves organized for the journey." Ms Woods nodded towards the red and black ship berthed at the main dock. "Pass up that gear, honey, and your little piggy. We have no time to waste."

OINKY OINKY NO-NO! Pig squealed, trotting to hide behind the tarpaulin. Pearly swivelled to face him, panic in her eyes.

"Are you perhaps a little deaf, honeybun?" said Ms Woods, poking out her perfect chin. "Pass that gear up, please. Hurry up."

OINKY OINKY NO-NO! OINKY OINKY NO-NO! Pig squealed and oinked and kicked his legs, making the dinghy rock.

Pearly didn't know what to do. She took a hesitant step back. The two burly men on either side of Ms Woods took a threatening step forwards.

Pearly drew in a fearful breath. They were monsters of men. Their rain jackets were stretched across vast

24

shoulders and mountainous biceps. Beneath their hoods, their bearded faces scowled at her. The taller of the two had a jagged scar from the corner of his eye to the edge of his beard. His top lip was pulled up into an angry sneer.

"I need to speak to my parents first," Pearly insisted as evenly as she could, resisting the urge to break into Italian.

"Well, honey, you can't," said Ms Woods, drawing out her vowels in a way that Pearly found highly annoying. She reached into her pocket and pulled out a piece of paper. "But I have this note from your father."

Pearly took the note. Was this a trick?

Pleese hand Little Pigggy to Ms Woods. Then go straighht home. Grandpa Esmerallda will be waitting.
Lov Daddy Woe x

The note was definitely in her father's handwriting. The letters were in his neat and careful hand, but the message had Pearly perplexed. It was riddled with spelling errors. Ricky Woe was not one for mistakes. And she never called him Daddy Woe, just as they never called Pig, Little Piggy. Either he wrote this under extreme stress or it was another warning. Or both.

OINKITY-SQUEALIO, oinked Pig. *DON'T TRUST HER!*

Pearly slipped the note into her raincoat pocket. "Don't worry, I don't," she whispered to Pig.

Oh, smoky bacon, what does it all mean? Worries exploded like fireworks in Pearly's head, making it impossible for her to think straight.

"So, what are you waiting for?" Ms Woods said, hands on her hips, those blue orbs peering down at Pearly. "You read what your father said – come on now, don't make a scene, hand over the little piggy."

I DON'T THINK SO, oinked Pig shrilly.

Pearly nodded to Pig. "I agree."

"Are you talking to that pig?"

"No! Of course not," said Pearly far too quickly.

"Then you agree to hand over the pig. Is that what you're saying, honey?"

"No. I am saying that I need to speak to my parents first." *And I don't trust anyone who calls me honey constantly, even if you are a movie star with the whitest teeth on earth!*

"I'm afraid that's just not possible, as I've already explained. You have the note. Hand over Little Piggy and then be on your way, home to your granny before she worries, and all."

Pearly licked her lips; her mouth was as dry as desert sand, and her skull seemed to have drums pounding away inside it. She couldn't hand over Pig, not to this woman.

Pig clicked his jaw and tapped his trotters, making a low and ominous sound. AROO. AROO. AROO. There was no direct translation to English, but Pearly knew that Pig was agitated and upset, and an agitated and upset Pig was best avoided.

Ms Woods gave an exasperated sigh. "You leave me no choice, I'm afraid, honeybun. Gaddi, Bernt. Get that lump of bacon and take him to the ship," Ms Woods instructed the giants, all sweetness gone from her voice.

It was the worst thing she could have said though, because as the two huge men stepped down onto the boat, Pig let out a furious grunt, scrambled onto the top of the tarpaulin and launched himself straight at them. He flew through the air, the black patches around his eyes making him look like some kind of masked bandit. A furious flying piggy masked bandit, in fact.

Kapow! Pig ploughed into the chest of one of the giants with such force that he toppled back into the other. The boat rocked dangerously. The men staggered sideways, then back, and then – kerplunk, splash – over the side.

Go Pig!

Pearly leaped to the bow of the dinghy and flipped the rope off the bollard. Time to make their escape.

But a piercing crack made her stop. She looked up, her skin prickling.

Ms Emmeline Woods stood on the end of the jetty, holding a long ugly pistol in both hands and wearing a smug gleam in her pretty blue eyes.

And Pig...

Pig was lying motionless at the back of the boat.

CHAPTER 5

"*Hai sparato Pig!*" *You shot Pig!* A scream came from deep within Pearly as she launched herself like a missile at Ms Woods, a fierce rage fuelling her leap to the jetty.

Ms Woods fended her off with ease and Pearly landed painfully on her backside.

"Don't get your bloomers all in a bother now, honeybun," said Ms Woods. "It's a tranquillizer gun. The pig's fine, but he'll be out for a few hours." She turned to face the two giants, who were climbing out of the river onto the jetty, water dripping from their bearded chins. "Do y'all think you might be able to handle the little piggy now?"

Pearly jumped back onto the boat and knelt beside Pig, stroking his white bristly hair. A long cylinder was stuck in his side and the sight of it made Pearly feel sick to the stomach. But he was breathing. Alive. And that was the most important thing.

The two giants clambered on board, muttering in a foreign language. Pearly's ears pricked up. She knew this language. It was a language that was particularly dear to her.

"Heimsk kona." Stupid woman.

"Já. Hvaða gagn er af svíni á skipi?" Yes. What use is a pig on a ship?

Icelandic – the language of her grandmother, Brigitta Helgadóttir, and the first of the twenty-six languages, other than English, that Pearly had learned since she uttered her first words.

Pearly kept her head down and tried to think. A seed of hope planted itself in her heart. Surely she could use this to her advantage and somehow rescue Pig – and her parents, who Pearly was now convinced needed rescuing too.

She stroked Pig and willed her brain to come up with a plan. But the sight of her motionless friend made her mind bubble with gruesome pictures. *Pig waking up and not recognizing her. Pig not being able to understand her any more. Pig being whisked away by helicopter for scientific experimentation. Pig not waking up at all...*

"Move," snarled the soggy giant with the scarred face, who was dripping all over her.

"We have to take him on the ship," said the other one, looking down at her with pleading eyes.

"Hurry up, you two!" yelled Ms Woods. "We set sail soon."

Pearly sat beside Pig unable to move, unable to think clearly. She knew that she was letting Pig down.

"Out of the way," said the scar-faced giant as two great hands the size of baseball mitts grabbed her under her arms and dragged her away from Pig's side.

"No!" sobbed Pearly.

The man shrugged.

He joined the other giant, and together they picked up Pig and awkwardly climbed out onto the jetty and waddled with him towards the ship.

Pearly watched them go, utterly devastated.

Ms Woods put her two fingers into her mouth and let fly with a sharp whistle.

Three more men appeared. "Get the gear," she ordered. "Hurry up!"

The three men jumped on board Pearly's dinghy and carried off the polar gear and her parents' adventure packs.

Tears tumbled down Pearly's cheeks. This was wrong, all wrong.

"Now, honeybun, go home to your grandma and let us get on with the job at hand." Ms Woods shook her wavy hair out of her eyes, turned and marched off after the men.

31

Pearly slumped against the side of the dinghy, her head in her hands.

She had failed.

Yet again.

CHAPTER 6

Why did she always do this? Why did she let her worries get in the way of clear thinking? How could she ever be an Adventurologist if she went to pieces at every obstacle? For the first time ever, her mother had said that they needed her – *We need you, Pearly* – and look how that had turned out. Pig had been shot by a white-toothed movie star and carried away by two bearded giants.

Pearly wiped her nose with her sleeve and peered up at the rusty bow of the icebreaker ship, rising high above the jetty, pointy like a weapon. She watched as the two Icelandic giants disappeared on board with Pig. Ms Woods and the other men were only a few steps behind them.

What was Pearly going to do? She couldn't go home – what was the point? There was no one there. Esmeralda wasn't going to appear suddenly from Singapore, and Grandpa Woe was visiting his cousins on the mainland in Sydney. One glance at her phone and she could see that the mobile network was still down, so she couldn't even call or text him.

She slid her phone back into her jacket pocket, and sighed a heavy sigh as she recalled her mother's warning: *Little Piggy's snout never lies.* Her strange messages had been puzzling and weird. What did the barn and shed mean?

And her father's note.

Pearly slipped it out of her pocket. It was a bit soggy now and some of the ink had run, but the message was still clear enough to read.

Pleese hand Little Pigggy to Ms Woods. Then go straighht home. Grandpa Esmerallda will be waitting. Lov Daddy Woe x

Two warning messages.

Two messages for her – *Pearly*.

Adventurologist in training. So many clues and she couldn't work out any of them. How could she be so gifted at languages and so dense about everything else?

And now her parents were relying on her. They were trusting her to be part of an adventure, even though she knew they probably didn't have a choice.

She couldn't let them down. She had to find them. Talk to them. See what it was that they needed her to do.

But to do that she had to get on board that ship. And in a hurry.

Pearly raced to the outboard engine at the back of the dinghy. It started on the first pull. She backed the dinghy out and away from the jetty and then headed off around the bend in the river, pointing the little boat towards Lemon Tree Passage and Woe Mansion, and hoping Ms Woods would think she had gone.

She could almost feel Ms Woods's blue eyes boring into her back. Was she watching from somewhere on board the *Mighty Muncher*? How on earth was she going to get on that boat? What would Ms Woods do to her if she caught her? Make her walk the plank? Feed her to her pet white pointer? Leave her on a deserted island with no food or water? And what if she was already too late? What if her parents were hurt? Is that why her father didn't deliver the message himself? Had Ms Woods used the tranquillizer gun on him? And maybe Angel too? Were they lying below deck somewhere unconscious? Or worse?

Pearly revved the little outboard motor, pushing the yellow dinghy faster and faster, and further downriver, away from Port Clementine. The weather was closing in again. The wind had dropped but the rain was pelting down, and a mixture of tears, snot and rainwater dripped off Pearly's chin.

She didn't know what to do! What if she never saw

her parents or Pig again? What if they needed her and she wasn't able to help? What if...

"Ferma!" Pearly yelled to the sky. *Stop!* She had to stop these thoughts that were sending her racing down the river and running away in a panic. She slowed the engine and glanced behind her. She was out of view of the ship now, so she turned the dinghy in a wide arc towards the riverbank, pulling in behind the cover of a cluster of mangroves.

She tied the dinghy to a fallen log and then collapsed onto the muddy ground, not caring that she had plonked herself into a huge puddle. Truth was, she felt like a puddle herself. A puddle of worries that were making her as useful as the puddle she was sitting in.

This was not part of a lesson from the *RAG*, or one of Grandpa Woe's morning challenges or her father's tests. This was real. Her parents needed her. Angel had said so. She had to do something. She couldn't just sit there and let her parents and Pig sail off to goodness knows where with that awful woman and her annoying accent, perfect teeth and tranquillizer gun.

Pearly willed herself to stand up. To step out of the puddle and do something. Anything.

Smoky bacon to those worries! Pig's voice said in her head. "Smoky Bacon" was a piggy way of cursing, and it was what Pig always said to her when she was letting her worries get in the way.

36

"Smoky bacon to those worries," Pearly whispered, and pushed herself out of the mud. "Smoky bacon to those worries," she said more loudly. "Bacon. Bacon. Bacon!" she screamed at the grey clouds and the muddy ground. As she peered through the mangroves up to the *Mighty Muncher*, she yelled, "Smoky bacon and pork chops to you too!"

She grabbed her adventure pack out of the dinghy, threw it over her shoulders and took off at a sprint.

She was going to rescue her parents and Pig too. That was all there was to it.

She had no time to lose.

CHAPTER 7

The rain had eased, but clouds were slung low across the sky, full of threat. Pearly slipped past the huge rusty barn-like buildings – warehouses, she guessed – that flanked the waterfront and walked purposefully towards the dock.

Standing beside the gangplank that led up to the *Mighty Muncher* was another bearded giant. Pearly was certain it wasn't Gaddi or Bernt. This giant's beard was like a bright orange tail of fizz, attached to his chin like a fox's tail. It reminded Pearly of her Icelandic grandmother's hair, her *amma*. Pearly crossed her toes inside her boots, hoping against hope that this giant was also from Iceland. Then she whispered *smoky bacon* three times under her breath and approached the orange-bearded man.

"Halló. Gott veður fyrir endur!" Hello. Good weather for ducks!

A grin broke out on the giant's face, revealing a

mouth full of broken teeth, like an ancient graveyard filled with crumbling tombstones. *"Íslensk?"* he questioned. *Icelandic?*

"No. My grandmother is though," replied Pearly in Icelandic. "My *amma*, Brigitta Helgadóttir, she makes sure we visit every second summer. I love Iceland."

Tears glistened in the man's icy blue eyes. "My name is Felix. I am very pleased to meet you." He held out his great hand and shook Pearly's fiercely, up and down, up and down, as Pearly introduced herself.

"I am pleased to meet you too," said Pearly. "There aren't many on Orchard Island who know anything about Iceland. Last summer *Amma* took me to see the northern lights. The colours! Swirling across the sky – yellow, blue, green. Nothing like it. It sent goosebumps down my spine. *Amma* makes the best spice cake you can imagine... Oh, just thinking about it makes me hungry. And then the glaciers and the icebergs sailing past, and everyone is so friendly." Her nerves were making her ramble.

"Oh, Pearly. How I miss it so," Felix said. "Your stories – they make homesickness in my heart. You are a true Icelandic storyteller."

"Actually, I think I got my stories from my mum – well, my mum's dad in particular. He's Italian. That's what *Amma* thinks anyway. She says I could talk under an ice lake if I needed to – once I get going, that is.

Sometimes I'm a little shy – I worry too much, you see, so I worry that I might be boring or say the wrong thing or too much or not enough..." Dang. More rambling. Pearly licked her lips and forced a smile.

Felix chuckled, deep and hearty like vegetable soup, his broken teeth wobbling in his mouth. "What a family. I have not seen my family for seven and a half months." Felix leaned against the rail, looking wistful.

"That must be hard," said Pearly, thoughts about her own family making sweat trickle down her back. "Which reminds me," she motioned to her adventure pack, "I have to take this on board for Ms Woods." Now that she had stopped her storytelling and was reminded of her true purpose, her voice crackled and she floundered like a fish on the shore. "It ... it ... it's for the trip ... to Antarctica."

"I will look after that for you. It will be my honour."

"Ah ... um ... thanks, but she said to hand it to her. I was meant to meet her on shore, but I was late. Can I hop on board and find her?"

Felix's eyes narrowed. His face filled with worry as he glanced up the gangplank and then back down to Pearly. "I'm not sure..."

"Please," said Pearly. "I want to make a good impression." The lie slipped out surprisingly easily. "I would love to travel with her one day."

"That is something that I would not recommend,"

Felix warned. "But, of course, hop aboard. And take a left up to the bridge – I am sure Ms Woods headed up there."

"Takk fyrir!" Thank you!

Pearly bounded up the gangplank. Gulls circled above her, dipping and swooping and squawking their mournful cries. To Pearly they sounded like warnings. Her legs were wobbly and her arms tingly. But she had done it. She was on board. Now to find her parents, so they could tell her what they wanted her to do, and so she could tell them about Pig. Once they knew what that Ms Emmeline Woods had done, there was no way they would stay on this ship! Pig was far too special for her parents to let Ms Woods get away with shooting him, even if she was a famous movie star.

CHAPTER 8

Pearly's boots clanged on the metal deck. CLANG. CLANG. CLANG. A sound like steel jaws snapping shut. A sound that made her think about the name of the ship: the *Mighty Muncher*. It wasn't a name that inspired confidence, that's for sure. *What does it munch?* she worried. *Ten-year-old girls who shouldn't be sneaking on board? Ten-year-old girls who should be heading home to their grandma, even though she is in Singapore?* In her imagination, the ship's bow became an enormous mouth with dagger teeth. It opened up and swallowed her whole, then spat out the bony bits it didn't like. She shook her head free of the image. *Mamma mia,* her imagination was a curse.

Pearly looked about nervously. There was no one to be seen on the narrow passageway that led off the gangplank, but she could hear some activity in the bow of the ship, where the bridge rose three storeys above her.

White painted guardrails.

Steel ladder-like steps.

Rows and rows of portholes.

A large grubby red chimney.

All looming over her. All daring her to step closer, so they could trip her up or fling her overboard. She turned to her right and took a few more steps. CLANG. CLANG. CLANG. She may as well have announced her arrival with a loudhailer. *Pearly Woe, here at your disposal. Don't mind me, I'm just here to tell my parents to get the heck off before they too get hit with a tranquillizer gun. If they haven't already been, that is.*

Up ahead, the passageway widened and a mechanical crane-like structure sat like a cat poised to strike a defenceless bird. Pearly pulled her hood closer around her face, kept her head down and headed towards the stern of the boat, hoping to find a way to get below deck.

And there it was. An oval-shaped steel hole and a set of stairs leading down.

Pearly was about to step through when she heard, CLANG CLANG CLANG. Footsteps. Approaching. In Pearly's mind's eye, she imagined one of the bearded giants, his mouth scowling, wolf claws extending out from the ends of his gnarly fingers. Her body tensed.

CLANG CLANG CLANG.

Pearly ducked through the doorway onto a landing, only moments before someone turned into the passageway. She slipped her adventure pack off her shoulders, then pressed her back against the metal wall, held her breath and sucked in her tummy.

CLANG CLANG CLANG. Closer. Closer still. She squeezed her eyes tight.

CLANG CLANG CLANG. Right outside the doorway now.

CLANG CLANG CLANG. And going right past.

Pearly let out her breath. That was close. She whispered "*Smoky bacon*" for courage, slung her adventure pack over one shoulder and tiptoed down the steep set of stairs and into another long corridor, which was lined with closed doors.

Fortunately, the corridor was deserted.

Unfortunately, as Pearly peered through the round windows on each door, the rooms also seemed deserted. Offices. Storerooms. Cabins with bunks lined against each wall. But no Angel or Ricky. And no Pig.

She diverted down another set of stairs and into an almost identical corridor. Except at one end of this corridor was a heavy metal door bulging with bolts and a wheel lock. Above the lock was a NO ENTRY sign, the words written in red. Pearly's heart skipped a beat. Maybe Pig was in there? But as she got closer, in smaller print the sign said ENGINE ROOMS. ENGINEERING STAFF ONLY.

Not a likely place to store a passed-out pig. Or fellow expedition passengers.

Pearly did an about-face and continued her search, looking through the windows in each door.

She had almost made it to the other end, when CLANG-CLANG-CLANG-CLANG – fast footsteps clomped down the stairs. Pearly turned the handle on the door beside her. It opened. She dived inside and pulled the door closed with a soft clink.

The smell that hit her nostrils nearly made her scream with excitement, but she managed to swallow it down, her hand clamped over her mouth as she listened to the footsteps. They seemed to be heading towards the engine room. Pearly heard the clunk-thud, thud-clunk of that heavy door unlocking, opening and then closing again.

Only then did Pearly give in to her excitement. She flicked the switch beside the door and the room was swamped with light. And, sure enough, just as Pig's snout never lies, her nose hadn't either. She knew she could smell her beloved Pig.

And there he was, in a too-small wire cage up against the far wall, lying on his side and still out cold. Pearly fell to her knees beside him, watching for the rise and fall of his chest.

She knew she should keep looking for her parents, but she couldn't tear herself away from Pig. Besides, the thought of being discovered by one of the crew sent terror zinging through her.

"Smoky bacon!" she hissed in Italian, more loudly than she should have. Pig shuddered. Pearly gazed at him, willing his eyes to open. But they remained shut.

The ship juddered and shook, and a loud mechanical growl filled her ears. The ship's engines were revving up. It was getting ready to set sail.

Pearly pushed herself off the floor. She had to find her parents and tell them about Ms Woods before the ship headed off to Antarctica. There was literally no time to lose now.

Pearly opened the door a crack and peered out. All clear.

She bolted down the corridor, her adventure pack bobbing against her back, panic making her bold as she threw open doors and checked inside the remaining rooms.

Her parents were definitely not on this level, or the one above. So that left the engine room – which was unlikely – or the levels above the main deck, where all the activity seemed to be. Could she slip up there without being seen?

A loud sound of scraping metal echoed through the passageway. Pearly rushed into an empty cabin and looked out of its tiny round porthole. The gangplank had been pulled up, and the stay ropes flung on board.

A whistle blasted and the ship groaned, the engines revving louder.

They were leaving!

CHAPTER 9

Pearly walked around in panicked circles. She muttered "*bacon, bacon, bacon*" in English, in Italian, in Pig. She held fistfuls of her hair and pulled hard. She couldn't think what to do.

But she had to do *something*, and quickly. The engines growled, a loud honk blasted and the ship rocked and pitched and moved away from the dock. Footsteps sounded on the floors above, orders were being shouted and there was a flurry of activity – some of it heading her way.

Pearly raced to Pig's cabin and leaped inside. She glanced around the room, taking proper notice this time. It was small – a storeroom of some sort. One wall was lined with shelves laden with all types of equipment: tents, sleeping bags, gloves, parkas, towels, all stacked neatly. The other wall housed picks and shovels and ropes and the like. Pig's cage was below the porthole wedged between the two shelved walls.

Pig hadn't moved, and Pearly's heart squeezed tight.

But right at that minute, she couldn't think about Pig. She needed a place to hide. A place to think and work out how best to find her parents, who she needed to find now more than ever.

She hurriedly rearranged the bottom shelf, which housed large green tent bags, and made a space for her to crawl behind them. She grabbed a couple of sleeping bags from the shelf above to pull on top of herself if need be; now at least she had a hidey-hole of sorts. Not the best place for a stowaway, which she now was, she realized, but it might buy her some time. As long as no one looked too carefully. Or needed a tent. Or a sleeping bag.

The ship was steaming steadily, the engines thrumming beneath her. Pearly leaned across Pig's cage to look out through the porthole. White water churned alongside the ship as it sliced its way through the grey waters. It was raining again, so already it was difficult to make out Port Clementine. Fingers of cloud crawled up the craggy cliffs that lined the shore; the grey warehouses along the dock were cloaked in mist and barely visible.

Pearly hid her adventure pack among the tent bags, plonked herself on the floor beside Pig and slid her arm through the bars of the cage. She scratched between his ears.

"Sorry, Pig," she said, sniffing back her tears. "This is all my fault. But I'll find Mum and Dad and they'll know what to do." What would her parents say when they discovered she was on board? She winced as she imagined that familiar look of disappointment on their faces. She stroked Pig's back. "Don't worry," she said.

She knew she was speaking for herself, not Pig. And she knew it was impossible for her not to worry. She worried about everything. She worried about accidentally murdering ants when she jogged through the apple orchard with her dad each afternoon. She worried about a stray speck of sugar eating holes in her teeth as she slept. She worried about her worries and how they would stop her from ever being an Adventurologist. So how could she stop worrying when her parents were missing, Pig had been shot, and she was a stowaway on a ship bound for Antarctica? She was worrying so much about worrying that when she heard footsteps in the passageway outside her door, she had only a split second to leap into her hidey-hole and pull the sleeping bags on top of her before the door was flung open.

"Still in la-la land," said a gruff male voice. "The Boss Lady will be happy."

"Who left the lights on?" said another, squeakier voice.

Mamma mia, thought Pearly and her pulse quickened. She'd forgotten about the light!

"Who cares?" said the gruff voice. There was the click of a switch and the cabin was sent into darkness. "Come on. Cook said supper will be ready in ten."

"*Já. Já.* I'm famished," said the squeaky voice.

The door closed and Pearly started breathing again.

She slipped out of her hiding spot and put her ear to the door, listening to the retreating footsteps.

Dinner time. That could well be the perfect time for her to recommence her search for her parents. She stretched her legs and let them hang out from the shelf between two tent bags. It was comfortable here. And safe. Sort of. Perhaps she should stay here for a bit and keep an eye on Pig.

Pig snorted in his sleep, startling Pearly and causing her to hit her head on the shelf above. She was such a clumsy klutz. *Tollpatsch.* (German.) *Ganso.* (Spanish.) *Hee-haw-haw-haw.* (Donkey.) *Gruntity-huff.* (Pig.)

She was stalling. Playing language games when really she should be doing something! No wonder her parents despaired at her ever being able to be an Adventurologist. She climbed out of her hidey-hole, rubbing her head and gazing at Pig, helpless in that cage.

No adventure too small, no challenge too great. That's what the Adventurologists' charter in the *RAG* stated. But the challenge ahead felt far too great for the likes of Pearly. Her shoulders slumped with the weight of it.

But with a fluttery stomach and a head fizzing with a million reasons not to, she edged open the door and tiptoed down the passageway, up two sets of stairs and onto the open deck. It was pouring again, which worked in her favour as the deck was deserted, except for a couple of gulls taking shelter under an overhang. Golden light shone from the rooms on the decks above her.

"Poi farlo," she told herself. *You can do it.* And she shakily climbed up to the next level.

Laughter erupted close by, and Pearly quickly turned herself into a human pancake, pressing herself against the wall. She closed her eyes and listened carefully. She could hear the scrape of cutlery on plates and the clink of glasses. This had to be the galley. There was much talking. Some people were speaking English, but in many different accents – French, Germanic, one possibly Norwegian and some others Icelandic. Pearly concentrated hard and tried to separate the voices. Her ear for language was her strength and maybe, just maybe, it might be helpful for once.

She picked off the voices one by one: gruff voice and squeaky voice complaining about the soup;

52

Felix with the red fox beard talking in Icelandic to the other two giants, Bernt and Gaddi, and one other she hadn't met yet; some giggly chatter in English about a drunken party on shore last night. Pearly slowed her breathing and listened harder, trying to locate Ms Woods's annoying twang. But either Ms Woods was too busy eating to talk, or she wasn't there. Sadly, it didn't seem as if Pearly's parents were there either. She would know those two voices anywhere, and if her mother was in there, she would be regaling everyone with one of her stories and making the whole room laugh.

Pearly ducked below the galley window and then tipped her head back to steal a glance inside. Eight or nine people sat around a long table, mostly men and maybe two women. A chubby man with colourful tattoos down both arms stood behind a serving bar. That confirmed it. Her parents were definitely not having dinner. Pearly popped back down and then tiptoed past the galley.

The next room was deserted. It looked like a common area, with sofas and low tables with maps and books strewn across them. Two computers stood on a long desk, their screensavers spiralling blue and green. Beside a large TV was a stairway that led up towards the bridge. On the opposite wall, an open door led to what looked like another passageway. Did she dare to go inside?

Pearly chewed at her fingernails as more laughter exploded from the galley. What choice did she have? She had to find her parents, and hiding below a window chewing her nails wasn't going to help her do that.

She whispered, "Smoky bacon to my worries," and slipped through the door.

Voices drifted down from the bridge, speaking English. Ms Woods and two others: one male, one female. It was official navigating-ship type of talk. Pearly headed for the door that led to the passageway.

"Keep that course. And be sure to pick up speed once we are out in open water. I'm getting my dinner now." It was Ms Woods, coming her way.

Pearly ducked behind an armchair. Ms Woods jogged down the stairs and out the door. Phew. That was close. But she would be back, that was for certain.

Pearly stepped out from behind the chair, but had only taken a couple of tentative steps towards the passageway when she heard someone else coming down the stairs. *Mamma mia!* This was impossible.

"Hang on a sec, Emmeline," called a snuffly male voice with a British accent. A person clattered down the stairs into the common room, sneezing loudly. Pearly didn't have time to get back to the chair, but noticed another door to her right. She pulled it open. It was a broom cupboard. She wasn't fond of tight spaces, but it would have to do. She stepped inside and closed the door. "We should take a few shots on the bridge while we're heading out. The light is delightfully soft and the rain's eased."

Pearly held her breath, the words "a few shots" making her heart pound.

CHAPTER 10

A prison. That's what this is, thought Pearly as she crept back into the storeroom where Pig's cage was. Pig was definitely a prisoner, and it was becoming increasingly likely that her parents were too.

This wasn't just Pearly imagining the worst. This was fact. This *was* the worst! And where did that leave Pearly? The thought sent shock waves down both arms.

It was now well after midnight and Pearly was dog-tired. She had spent hours stuck in the dark of that broom cupboard, pushing down waves of panic about being in such a small space. Wet mop fronds had tickled her nose, and broom handles had stuck into her ribs. The smell of damp and disinfectant had made her nauseous. But it was worth every miserable second, because while she stood rigid with fear, sweat dripping from her chin and down her back, petrified she would be discovered, she was able to listen to the crew's conversations as they loafed about the common room after dinner. And that had given her something precious – information. Grandpa Woe always said that knowledge was power. He had written about it in the *RAG*. And right now, she needed all the power she could rustle up.

The Icelandic conversations were particularly useful – and often funny. At times Pearly had to muffle her laughter at their insults about Ms Woods. The "Boss Lady" they called her behind her back, with a mocking sneer in their voices. She was not at all popular. The Boss Lady was a *complete fool* according to Bernt and Gaddi. She had *no idea* how to run a ship, jeered Felix. Everyone agreed. Apparently she spent too much time putting on lipstick, taking selfies and posing for Stanley Snell. Stanley, Pearly worked out, was the man with the British accent who had called out to Ms Woods, and Pearly was relieved to deduce that the shots he was talking about were photos, not gunshots. The crew had nicknamed him "The Sneeze", and much time was given to thinking up pranks the crew could play on him and Ms Woods, most resulting in them both being hurled overboard into the mouths of waiting sea lions. This was important information – knowledge that could possibly give Pearly some power; some advantage. Maybe.

Ms Woods and Stanley "The Sneeze" Snell didn't hang out with the crew, but Ms Woods clomped through the common room a couple of times shouting orders or complaining about jobs not done to her satisfaction. Her voice had totally lost its honey, but not its American twang. Stanley retired early, after a sneezing and coughing fit – which totally explained his nickname – saying his hayfever was playing up and he had to be up at dawn for a photo shoot with Ms Woods. She *had* to be a movie star. Why else would she have a photographer on board? But why would a movie star want to kidnap Pig, and possibly Pearly's parents, and track the Great Hairy Beast? Something didn't add up.

The rest of the conversations were about family and parties and the thrill of finding the ice floes and entering Antarctic waters. One woman with a European accent seemed to be talking to her family via a video link on one of the computers. And there were a few whispered mutterings about Pig – mostly poking fun at Ms Woods for bringing a pig on such an expedition – but there was not one mention of Pearly's parents. Not one. Nor did she hear their voices. This twisted Pearly's guts into knots. In her mind, her parents were tied and gagged and locked in a tiny cabin with no food or water. She imagined poisonous tranquillizer darts sticking out from their thighs, their breathing shallow, their brows beaded with sweat. It was an image she couldn't shift and one that made her mother's words ring through her head all the more urgently: *We need you, Pearly.*

Once the room had fallen silent, Pearly had edged open the door, crept out of the cupboard and tiptoed down the corridor. Fluorescent tubes lit the echoey passageways and this made Pearly feel way too present. Twice she had to grip the handrail to steady herself as the ship swayed and rocked in the open sea. Some of the doors along the passageway were closed and had their blinds down. Pearly guessed these were sleeping quarters. Some with doors open seemed to be offices, others empty cabins. The ship definitely wasn't full of passengers. There was a skeleton crew, Ms "I'm so famous" Woods and The Sneeze, it appeared.

Pearly snuck into a bathroom – she was busting – then she explored the outer decks, creeping from shadow to shadow. She found nothing except large yellow shipping containers, padlocked shut, and billowing tarps tied over vehicles and equipment.

As Pearly was trying to peer under one of the tarps, a crew member appeared out of the shadows, startling Pearly. She got such a fright she hurriedly returned to Pig.

Now she lay beside him, watching his belly rise and fall. Her heart swelled with love as her stomach tightened with worry. It had been hours since Ms Woods had shot him with that dart and he was still out cold. He looked so vulnerable, lying within the wire cage, and Pearly was oddly grateful that he was unconscious and didn't know that he had been pig-napped.

Pearly laid her hand on his chest to reassure herself that he was indeed breathing, and a sour taste rose into her mouth as memories came rushing in of the time she had done exactly the same thing to Grandpa Woe.

It was a horrible memory. A nightmarish memory. Grandpa Woe had fallen from a horse on an adventure in the outback on the mainland. He had hit his head and been airlifted all the way to Orchard Island Hospital, where he had lain motionless in a coma for weeks, just like Pig was now. Esmeralda had flown in from Singapore – despite the fact they'd been divorced for years – and had insisted that someone be beside him at all times, talking to him, coaxing him out of his coma, telling him how much he was loved and needed. The doctors had all given up, but Esmeralda wouldn't have it, and neither would Grandpa Woe apparently, because after seven weeks of nothing, he woke suddenly and announced that he would like to go home to Woe Mansion – and hurry up about it!

Pearly willed Pig not to give up and to wake up *right now*, like Grandpa Woe had.

She would make sure he would, she decided. She'd do the same as Esmeralda had done. She'd talk Pig's pink ears off, if that's what it took.

"Come on, Pig. Wake up," Pearly crooned, her face pressed to the cold wire of the cage. "I can't possibly go on without you. Please, please wake up."

She bit her lip and willed away the tears, trying to remember the types of things Esmeralda had said to Grandpa Woe. Some of them were soppy and surprisingly lovey-dovey, she recalled. Pearly even wondered how truthful they were, seeing as Esmeralda and Grandpa Woe were divorced and had to live in different countries to avoid World War III – or so her mum had told her.

"Remember ... remember," Pearly searched her brain for ideas, "remember when I was little and I rode on your back and we trotted all over the place, until we fell down that old sinkhole. I thought we were doomed. But you didn't give up, Pig. No, you oinked and oinked until Mum found us. Don't give up now. Please.

"Remember all the good times we've had – like when we played secret missions ... and hiding in the apple orchard." Pearly sniffed and wiped her nose on her jacket. Pig hadn't even twitched. "OK, how about a deal? If you wake up, I promise to admit that you are the corn fritter eating champion, and the best at burping *and* at cliff-climbing races. I don't know how you do that, with those trotters. How do you get up that cliff so fast?"

Pearly scratched around Pig's ears. She rested her head in the crook of one arm and continued with a sigh. "Who will I talk to if you don't wake up, huh? Who? I know Mum and Dad think it's strange how we can communicate – remember how they were so weird about it, making it into some big deep dark family secret, as if they were ashamed of it? They've told no one, not even the Guild. But can you remember a time when we couldn't? I feel like I could always understand you, and you definitely understand me better than anyone else.

"Come *on*, Pig. Wake up, please. I need you more than ever. I can't see a way out of this mess without your help. I need your support *and* your snout. I can't find Mum and Dad anywhere. Your snout is bound to be able to find them – it is extraordinary, far more extraordinary than my language talent. It's as if you possess some kind of magical power..."

It sounded weird to Pearly, saying that out loud. It was something she had thought about often, but had never been brave enough to talk about. It was all a little woo-woo for her logical father and practical mother. But there was no denying that Pig's snout was remarkable. So remarkable that it seemed as if it *was* magical. Who else could identify every animal on the planet from hundreds of metres away? Who else had a snout that could sniff out trouble and never get it wrong? Pearly wondered if it had something to do with Pig's mother – the Divine Sow of the Kingdom of Anachak.

"Do you miss her, Pig?" Pearly whispered. "Your mother? I've never asked before, because I didn't want to know the answer. But do you ever wish you were back in the jungles near that mighty Mekong River? I know it's selfish, but I hope you don't. I sometimes wonder what would have happened if Mum and Dad hadn't found the king's son in that cave, and if the king hadn't gifted you to us to say thank you. What would my life be like then? Without you – my one and only magical bestie?"

Pearly sat bolt upright, struck rigid by a thought as powerful and as dangerous as lightning. What if Ms Woods had found out about Pig's special power? What if she was only pretending to be looking for the Great Hairy Beast? What if it was Pig that she really wanted? It made perfect sense – why else would she want Pig to come along? What use was a pig in Antarctica? What use was a pig to someone famous unless it was an extraordinary pig with an extraordinary power? Maybe they weren't even going to Antarctica.

Pearly had heard of famous movie stars who made great demands and got whatever they wanted. Maybe Ms Woods wanted to own Pig. Maybe she used the Great Hairy Beast to lure Pearly's parents to the dock. Maybe she tried to buy Pig, and when Pearly's parents refused...

Panicked, Pearly reached one arm into the cage and rested it on Pig's back. His bristly warmth was reassuring. "Please wake up, Pig! Please," she whispered. "I think you're in grave danger and so are Mum and Dad."

Mamma mia! Questo è terribile.

This was more than a sticky situation – this was superglue sticky, the type that you can't unstick. In other words – impossible.

Pearly had never felt so alone.

Alone and out of her depth.

She stroked between Pig's ears, and then laid her head back in the crook of her other arm. Her stomach gurgled with hunger and her mouth was dry from thirst, but she didn't have the energy to reach for her adventure pack. She was too tired.

Within seconds, poor exhausted Pearly fell into a deep sleep.

CHAPTER 11

The sun was warm on Pearly's face. A gentle breeze teased her curls. She moulded a lump of sticky mud with both hands into a pie shape. She rolled another lump into a twisty snake to coil on top. Her mud pie was a masterpiece – far better than Pig's. Which wasn't surprising, because trotters weren't cut out for shaping pies.

A voice drifted down to her. It was her mother calling out from the top of the steep stairs cut into the cliff that led from the riverbank up to Woe Mansion.

"Pizza is ready," *Pearly told Pig.*

Race you! *grunted Pig, and he scuttled up the stairs.*

Pearly hadn't taken one step before she fell to the ground, a sharp pain in her ribs.

"What, might I ask, are you doing here?" A smooth voice with a nasally twang startled her awake, and she opened her eyes in time to see the pointy toe of a high-heeled boot jab her in the ribs.

"A stowaway. Are you kidding me? Really?" Pearly squinted up at Ms Woods's tanned face, her red-lipsticked lips curled into a snarl over those dazzling teeth, and she remembered where she was.

"Get up, honeybun, and explain yourself."

Pearly stumbled to her feet, fear creeping over her.

"I ... I ... ju ... just wanted to talk to Mum and Dad. I ... I ... didn't mean ... to stow away. The ship left before I ... I ... found them."

Ms Woods drew in a deep, agitated breath. "You stupid, stupid girl. What are we meant to do with you now?"

Throw me into the tentacle arms of a giant octopus? Drop me off in a tiny inflatable dinghy with no food or water or life vest? "T ... take me to Mum and Dad?" she tried. "Please? They'll know what to do."

"Will they? I'm not so sure about that." Ms Woods ran her tongue over her teeth, then sniggered a breathy snigger through her nose. It made Pearly wince. What did she mean?

"Please!" Pearly begged. "Let me see them."

"That is not going to happen, so you may as well forget it, you hear?"

"I ... I..."

"Close that gaping mouth of yours before you swallow a fly, and get used to the fact that you are not going to get your own way around here. No siree!

66

You can stay locked up with the pig for now." Ms Woods glanced at her wristwatch and then at Pig. She pinched her chin with her thumb and forefinger, and narrowed her eyes. "Has he come to yet?" she asked.

Pearly shook her head.

"Mmmm. Not good." She turned to leave. "He's your responsibility. You make sure he is awake and alert before I return. Got it? If he's not, well..." Ms Woods bent her head to one side and smiled.

"Well, what?" croaked Pearly.

"I don't think I need to spell it out, do I, honeybun? I will not be happy, that's what, and that won't be good for you. Got it?"

Pearly grimaced and nodded.

"Felix," Ms Woods yelled. "Stand guard outside this door. Don't let this little stowaway out, no matter what."

The orange-bearded Felix appeared in the doorway. "Yes, ma'am." He kept his eyes downcast as he spoke.

"But Mum? Dad?" Pearly tried again as a man who Pearly suspected was Stanley Snell appeared beside Ms Woods. He sniffled and then sneezed – confirming her suspicions – as he swung an impressive-looking camera around a thick wobbly neck made up of layer upon layer of chins.

"There you are, Emmeline dear. We should get those journey sho—" He stopped mid-sentence as he noticed Pearly on the ground. Puffy eyes in a beach ball face went from Pearly to Pig and back to Pearly. He pulled out a hanky and wiped his nose roughly. "Emmeline, what's this about?"

"A small distraction," Ms Woods replied, flicking her hand at Pearly as if she was a speck of dirt. Stanley harrumphed. He didn't look too pleased. "I'll get my other coat and I'll meet you up on the forward deck." She turned to Felix. "You know what to do, yes?"

Felix gave a quick nod. Ms Woods and Stanley left. Felix followed them out and pulled the door shut behind him, still not making eye contact with Pearly.

Pearly tried the handle. The door was locked. She sat on the floor and leaned back against the door, legs outstretched and eyes closed against threatening tears. How could one person mess things up so badly? So far she had only succeeded in getting everyone into more trouble.

Just then, Pig gave a violent convulsion. Pearly's heart nearly broke out of her chest. She bit her lip and held her breath. Pig kicked his back legs out. He snorted. He grunted. He oinked in a muttering way, *Smoky bacon and pork chops,* and then sprang up, his legs unsure and decidedly wobbly on the wire floor of the cage.

"Pig!" Pearly yelled, and leaped to his side. "Are you OK?"

OINKY OINKY NO-NO! Pig oinked. *TROUBLE. I SMELL TROUBLE.* OINKY OINKY NO-NO! OINKY OINKY NO-NO!

Pig shook himself vigorously and then grunted. *Of course, I am,* he oinked. *But where the heck are we and why do you look so terrible?*

"It's a long story," Pearly said as she crossed her legs and sat beside Pig, feeling a tiny seed of hope for the first time since yesterday, when the Adventure Phone had rung back in Woe Mansion. "I messed up big-time and now I think we're all in danger. Boy, am I glad you're OK. We are going to need a Grandpa-Woe-style plan to get out of this mess!"

CHAPTER 12

The *Mighty Muncher* pitched and rolled and swayed so much that it felt as if the ship was caught in the swirl of a washing machine, rather than sailing across the Southern Ocean.

Pearly tried to ignore her nausea as she swayed in time with the ship. She held the soggy, crumpled note her father had written and read it again to Pig.

Pleese hand Little Pigggy to Ms Woods. Then go straighht home. Grandpa Esmerallda will be waitting. Lov Daddy Woe x

Strange, Pig oinked. *You say that it's wrong? That the spelling is wrong? Whatever that is.*

Pig *was* extraordinary, there was no doubt about it. He could understand English, sniff out trouble and any animal species known to man, and he could speak Pig in a way Pearly could understand – but he just didn't get written language at all. Pearly had given up trying to explain English spelling to him long ago. It was hard enough for a fairly intelligent human girl with a talent for languages to understand, let alone a pig from the jungles along the Mekong. Even an extraordinary one.

"Yes," replied Pearly. "There are extra letters and some wrong letters and a missing one too – and the message doesn't make sense. Especially when you put it with Mum's messages."

Pig grunted and snorted with frustration. *What letters are wrong? Does that make a difference?* Pig oinked. *Maybe it is like one of those codes Grandpa Woe gives you for your morning challenge.*

Yes! Why hadn't she thought of that? Pig may not understand English spelling but he *was* definitely brilliant. Pearly shuffled through her adventure pack until she had retrieved her pencil and notebook. Then she carefully wrote down all the wrong letters from the note:

E G H P L T and E (missing)

Pearly stared at the letters. What did they mean? Was it a code? A puzzle? She tried rearranging them into a word. She sucked on her lips, her tongue poking out to one side in concentration.

PLEEGTH
PLEGEHT
THEPEGL
GLEETHP

Well? Any luck? oinked Pig.

Pearly shook her head, changed sides with her tongue, and added the mistakes from her mum's messages to her list.

1. Little Piggy instead of Pig.
2. Grandma instead of Esmeralda.
3. Grandma looking after her when she was actually in Singapore.
4. The shed in the big barn by the water's edge.

She looked back to her father's note and then added the strange way he had signed off to the list.

5. Daddy Woe instead of Dad or Ricky.

What did it all mean?

She went back to the letters. It had to be a coded message. If only she could see it.

THE PLEG
THE GLEP
THE GELP
TEG HELP

Hold on! Blood rushed into Pearly's head as the letters rearranged themselves into: GET HELP.

"Oh, Pig. GET HELP – that's what the message is. Mum and Dad *are* in trouble! They were, right from the beginning!" Pearly couldn't hold back the tears now. Her worst fears were confirmed. Her parents were in trouble and they were relying on Pearly to help.

Some help *she* was – locked in a storeroom on a

ship in the middle of the ocean. How was she going to get help now?

She wanted to wail. To bang her feet against the linoleum floor. But her tantrum didn't even have time to start, because Pig oinked, *HUMAN APPROACHING!*

The lock clicked and the door handle turned.

Pearly drew in her breath and backed up against the cage, shoving the note into her pocket, just as the door opened and Felix trudged in.

He thrust a tray with a bowl and a bottle of water at Pearly, still not looking at her. "Here," he said. "And take it easy. This might be it for the day. Depends on my mood." There was a nasty scowl to his voice, and Pearly wondered where the good-natured, belly-laughing Felix had gone.

"Thank you," she said in Icelandic, as she stood and took the tray.

"Don't start thinking you can charm me by speaking Icelandic," Felix snarled, his graveyard teeth seemingly rattling around in his mouth. "Won't fall for that trick again." He straightened his shoulders and loomed over her. He *was* a giant.

Pearly gulped. "I wasn't tricking," Pearly said, still speaking Icelandic. "I was ... I was..."

"Lying? Is that what you are trying to say? *I just need to deliver this pack to Ms Woods,*" he said in a mocking tone, mimicking Pearly. "Yeah, right. And speak

English, liar, you are a blight on the Icelandic people – lucky for me the Boss Lady hasn't worked out how you got on board, but once she does..." He didn't finish. Instead, he turned his back on Pearly and stepped through the doorway.

"Wait!" cried Pearly. "I need your help."

"Ha! That's rich. You need *my* help – you who tricked me. That could see me thrown off the ship, you know!" The ship swayed and pitched and Pearly stumbled towards Felix. He caught her by the arm and flung her back towards Pig's cage. Pig snorted with disgust.

"Ah, the little piggy is awake. The Boss Lady will be happy." Felix turned to leave again.

"Felix, please wait. I am really sorry I tricked you. But my parents are in trouble. That's why I snuck on board. I think Ms Woods has kidnapped them." She didn't really know if she could trust Felix, but she didn't have many other options. "Please, please help me. I need to find them."

Felix hesitated. "And why would I believe anything that comes out of that lying mouth of yours?"

Pearly hung her head in despair. "I don't know," she whispered, looking up at Felix. "But I do know that you don't like Ms Woods – that you would all like to throw her and Stanley 'The Sneeze' Snell into the mouths of waiting sea lions." Pearly crossed her fingers behind her back. *Information is power.* She hoped Grandpa Woe was right.

Felix narrowed his eyes at Pearly, then closed the door gently behind him. "How do you know that?"

"I was hiding in the broom cupboard when you were all in the common room last night."

"You little eavesdropping sneak, you—"

"I was looking for my parents and got stuck in there. Please, Felix, I really need your help. My parents wrote me a coded message asking me to help them and I can't even find them, let alone help them and now Pig has been snatched and I don't know what to do, especially as I'm locked in here and—"

"Stop! Stop! You better not be telling me porkies."

Pig snorted at the word "porkies" – it wasn't a favourite of his – but Pearly put her hands to her chest and looked up at the man earnestly. "I cross my heart," she said. "I fear my parents are in danger. Can you please see if you can find them? That's all – I just need to know where Ms Woods has them. I've already tried but I failed."

Felix regarded her for a long moment, pulling at the red fox tail on his chin. "Ha! You think me a fool, don't you?" He tramped out and locked the door behind him – the click of the lock punctuating the fact that Pearly had probably just lost the one ally she had on board.

CHAPTER 13

Pearly watched the churning sea from the tiny porthole above Pig's cage. The waves were mountainous. The icebreaker rode up then down, up then down, as if on a mighty rollercoaster. It made her insides churn, and she was grateful that her stomach was more or less empty.

Pearly climbed back down from the window and slumped cross-legged beside Pig. She took a swig from the water bottle and fed Pig another mouthful of the tasteless porridge Felix had brought them.

What I'd give for one of your mum's corn fritters or veggie pizzas right now, Pig oinked as he rolled the gruel around in his mouth, his pink piggy eyes closed as if savouring the memory.

"That's not likely." Pearly sighed. She took another sip of water in an effort to settle her gurgling stomach as the *Mighty Muncher* crashed down another rollercoaster wave, sending so much spray up past their porthole that she ducked instinctively.

It had been hours since Felix had stomped out, and Pearly was growing more and more anxious with each passing minute. She'd blown it, for sure. She imagined Felix pulling on his foxy beard and laughing with the famous Ms Emmeline Woods as he told her about the pathetic stowaway begging him to find her parents. She imagined Ms Woods fixing her make-up before storming down to wherever her parents were being held, her boots clomping on the metal floor, and ordering Gaddi and Bernt to toss them into an airless dungeon in the belly of the ship. She imagined them starving and thirsty and sick with worry about her and Pig.

Her stomach lurched at that thought, and bubbles of nausea rose up into her throat. She burped them down and fed Pig another mouthful of the porridge, then curled onto the floor beside him.

She had to come up with a plan. Plan A was obviously a dismal failure. She needed to focus on her training, like Grandpa Woe always told her to. She needed to conjure up pages from the *RAG* that might help her. If only she had thought to bring it with her. Surely there was something useful she could remember from her three long years of training. She wasn't a good student, but she *had* been a student, she *had* learned stuff – she should know *something*! But instead of pages from the *RAG*, her mind kept filling with images of that dungeon and her parents' limp bodies, shadowy lumps in the darkness.

Pig spluttered and almost choked on his porridge, startling her out of her imaginings. OINKY OINKY NO-NO! he oinked. *Human approaching! The red-bearded Icelandic one.*

Pearly sat herself up, eyes wide with anticipation.

The sharp click of the lock made her gasp as the door creaked open. Felix slipped in and closed the door softly behind him. He was carrying another tray with a plastic tub of water, a bowl of vegetable peelings and mouldy scraps for Pig, and a plate with a bacon sandwich on it.

The smell of the bacon wafted around the small cabin and Pig started AROO-AROO-AROOing. Understandably, bacon made him stressed.

Felix drew his bushy red eyebrows together and pulled a face at Pig's aggression. "Is he vicious?" he asked, putting the tray on one of the shelves and keeping his distance.

"It's the bacon," Pearly explained. "He gets agitated when he sees relatives being people's food. Perhaps put the sandwich outside?"

Felix rolled his eyes, but he put the sandwich plate on the floor outside the room and came back in.

Pearly's mouth was dry and her hands trembled at her sides. "Did you ... did you look ... look for my parents?" she whispered.

"Hush. Be quiet!" Felix hissed in Icelandic.

"And speak Icelandic." He peered behind him, as if to check if anyone was listening from the hall, then he leaned closer to Pearly. "I'm not sure why, I have to say, maybe it's because of your *amma* and your stories of her spice cake, but against my better judgement, I searched for your parents – top to bottom, every cabin, every corner. I checked the ship's log and made a few discreet enquiries. And I can assure you that there is no one on this ship except the crew, the Boss Lady, The Sneeze, the Pig and you, the stowaway. No one else. So either you are telling me porkies—" Pig *AROO*ed and kicked his legs out. Felix frowned at him and continued. "Either you are telling me … *lies* again … sending me on a wild puffin chase or..." He paused, pulling at his beard.

"Or what?" Pearly asked.

"Or your parents have been left behind. Because they are definitely not on board this ship. And now I am out of here and don't you dare ask for my help again. I mean it."

Felix left.

Pearly crumpled to the floor.

No. This couldn't be right. It had to be a mistake.

Because this was worse, far worse than any of her imaginings!

CHAPTER 14

Her parents were in trouble.

And they weren't on the ship.

They needed Pearly's help – her mother had even said so. *We need you, Pearly.*

And so had her father. *GET HELP.*

And where was Pearly?

Locked in a storeroom with Pig in a cage, on board an icebreaker ship in the middle of the Southern Ocean and probably halfway to Antarctica by now!

She was tired. She was both hungry and seasick. And she was dying to go to the loo. She couldn't even help herself, let alone Pig or her parents. She was as useful as a bikini in a snowstorm. She would never be an Adventurologist – she wasn't made of the right stuff.

And now she may never see her parents again. And Pig may end up being Ms Woods's little pet for ever. Or maybe even dinner. Who knew what she wanted with him? But it was clear that she wanted him.

She lay curled on the floor, muttering *smoky bacon* over and over in all twenty-seven languages that she had mastered so far. Pig paced in his cage – which was hard, as the cage was only marginally larger than Pig, so it was more like on-the-spot tramping. Every now and then he AROOed in frustration, like a wolf howling at the moon.

And that only made Pearly feel worse.

AROOOOOO. AROOOOOO. Pig gave one extra super loud AROOOOOOOOOOO. Then he stopped pacing and started oinking. OINKY OINKY NO-NO! OINKY OINKY NO-NO!

Pearly lifted her head ever so slightly off the floor – it felt too heavy to lift any higher. "Trouble?" she croaked. "*More* trouble? Where?"

Right here in this room, oinked Pig.

Pearly pushed herself up and swivelled on her backside to face Pig. "In here?" Her eyes flitted around the room. Her body tensed. "Where? What?"

I'm looking at it.

Pearly looked to either side of where she was sitting, then back at Pig, whose pink piggy eyes were trained directly on her. "Who? Me?"

Yes. You. You and your "I'm no good. I'm a big fat failure. Why did my parents pick me to help..." Pig mimicked Pearly's whiny tone to perfection.

"I never said any of those things. How do you know what I was thinking? That's spooky, even for you."

It's all over your face. And the way you were curling up on the floor like a decaying corn cob. Think I like it here? I need to get out of this cage – it stinks, in case you hadn't noticed. And you need to pull yourself together.

Pearly hung her head. Pig was right, and she felt ashamed. And now that he mentioned it, it did stink in here, which only made her nausea rise up into her throat again. She swallowed it down.

So, continued Pig, *Ricky and Angel are not on board. So where are they?*

"I don't know! That's the problem."

Think! Stop wallowing – that's for pigs. When you talked to Angel last, where did she say she was?

"At … at the dock. Ms Woods was with her – I could hear her grumbling in the background." Pearly shuffled on her backside to her adventure pack and pulled out the notebook where she had deciphered her father's message. Pearly scanned her notes. Maybe there was a clue there she had missed before.

1. Little Piggy instead of Pig.
2. Grandma instead of Esmeralda.
3. Grandma looking after her when she was actually in Singapore.
4. The shed in the big barn by the water's edge.
5. Daddy Woe instead of Dad or Ricky.

"This one – about the barn and the shed. That has to be it. I was confused at the time because we don't have a barn..."

Were there any barns at the port?

"No," Pearly said grimly. "It's a port, not a farm." She tried to recall the port area, what she'd seen as she made that dash to the *Mighty Muncher*. "There were lots of buildings, and trucks and – wait! Hang on. The warehouses! The warehouses along the waterfront. I remember thinking that they looked like big barns. Oh, Pig, I'm so stupid – why didn't I realize before: *the big barn by the water's edge*. I might have walked right past my own parents when I snuck on board. They were counting on me to help them! This is beyond terrible."

Pearly could see it clearly: Ricky and Angel tied up in a dank room – *the shed* – at the back of one of those warehouses. It all fit. Ms Woods must have locked them in. There was no way her parents would send those messages to Pearly and put her and Pig in danger unless they themselves were in extreme danger. *GET HELP.* It was so simple. So obvious. And she had missed it. They needed her to get help – not sail off on a ship to Antarctica!

Were they alone? Had Ms Woods tied them up and just left them? How could Pearly *GET HELP* now that she was probably hundreds of kilometres away?

She tried to visualize the pages from the *RAG*. She tried to channel Grandpa Woe's wisdom. She tried to recall the lessons Ricky had given her and the training sessions with Angel.

"Pig, you have to help me. What are some of the things to remember about Sticky Situations?"

Expect the unexpected, Pig oinked.

"I guess this is unexpected – so I probably should have expected it. But I don't think that's going to help now."

Pig did the snorty grunt he did when he was thinking. *What about: make the impossible, possible.*

"Helping my parents when I'm so far away is definitely impossible. But how do I make it possible? How do I *GET HELP* now I'm..." Pearly jumped to her feet. "A message. I need to send a message to the coastguard or the police or someone on Orchard Island!"

Pig squealed. *Where's your phone?*

Pearly hit her forehead with the heel of her hand – sometimes she was so stupid that it surprised even her. Again, so simple. *She* could phone for help. She pulled her phone out of her jacket pocket. *Smoky bacon!* It was dead. If only she had tried this earlier. "There must be a radio or phone somewhere I can use. Or maybe one of the computers in the common room. I heard one of the crew talking to her family on a video call last night."

She had to act fast. She banged against the door. "Felix!" she yelled. "I need you."

There was no response. She banged again. How could she get Felix to open the door?

"Felix, please! I think I'm ... I'm ... erm ... going to vomit!" she lied. "Please let me out. Felix?"

Still no answer. Pearly pulled up the roller blind in the middle of the door and squashed her face against the window to see if she could see anyone outside. "I don't think he's there."

Pig held his nose to the air. *Yes he is. His scent is strong.*

Pearly banged and kicked at the door. "Please! I'm sick! I need the toilet." She banged fiercely just as the door swung open, the force of it throwing her to the floor.

"What's all the racket for?" Felix asked.

"I need the toilet. I'm sick," Pearly said.

Felix's eyes sparkled and his belly laugh filled the small room. "Ha! You are not the only one. The Boss Lady, she has had her head in a bucket all day. And the cook! Hurry up, then. There's a toilet in the cabin next door."

Pearly fled out of the door and into the bathroom. She had been using her nausea as an excuse, but as soon as she entered the bathroom, Pearly was consumed by the violent urge to throw up, which she did, quite spectacularly, into the toilet bowl. Once her stomach had settled, she flushed it all away, then relieved her aching bladder, washed her face and hands, and slipped back to her prison, where Felix was waiting. She glanced at his jacket pockets and wondered if he had a mobile phone on him.

Felix placed a bucket at her feet. "For all your business – if you know what I mean."

Pearly knew exactly what he meant and she was not impressed, but she tried not to show it. She had more pressing concerns.

"Felix," she said, her voice soft but urgent. "I need your help."

"Forget it. I meant what I said." He turned to leave.

"Wait! Please. I've worked it out. I think my parents are being held captive in one of the warehouses at Port Clementine. They told me to get help but I blew it. Now I realize they're still there and need my help more than ever. I have to radio a message to the coastguard or police or someone. Can you help me? Do you have a phone? Can you use the radio?"

Felix levelled his gaze at Pearly. Pearly couldn't read his expression. Then he looked away and stepped towards the door, his head bowed. "Na. Na. You ask too much. I have done enough," he told her, his eyes trained to the floor again. "My job on this ship, it is already in jeopardy because of you."

The clanging of boots on metal stairs made both Pearly and Felix whip their heads around to face the open door.

Felix's face turned almost as red as his beard. He walked around in an agitated circle. "You are unbelievable!" he shouted loudly, waving his arms about violently and causing Pearly to jump out of his way. "Trouble. That's what you are. Nothing but trouble, with a capital T."

Human outside, oinked Pig from his cage.

Pearly glanced anxiously at Pig, then back at Felix. "Please," she kept her voice soft, "my parents' lives depend on it."

"No," Felix replied softly. He stomped out. "Ya, ya! Nothing but trouble," he said in Icelandic to whoever was outside. "The stowaway, she is a big pest – like a festering boil on the butt. I hope the Boss Lady gets rid of her soon. Before I turn white-haired like an old man."

The door closed.

Pearly tensed as she waited for the dreaded click of the lock.

But there was no click.

Pearly looked at Pig, a nervous, but hopeful grin spreading across her face.

CHAPTER 15

Had Felix forgotten to lock the door because someone had been outside and distracted him? Or had he left it unlocked on purpose? Pearly had no idea. But it was night-time now – had been for several hours – and part of Pearly was itching to turn that handle and slip out and try to get help somehow.

Unfortunately, the other part of Pearly couldn't stop thinking about all the awful things that might happen if she got caught.

Maybe I'll be left on top of a craggy cliff on a deserted island, with hungry grey vultures circling overhead. Maybe Ms Woods will turn Pig into pork chops and spicy spare ribs for the crew!

That part of Pearly wanted to slide onto the hidey-hole bed she had made and take a nice long nap. And *that* Pearly – Pearly the worrier – was winning.

Now or never, oinked Pig. *Now or never!* He was doing his on-the-spot pacing again. Pearly sensed he would be AROOing at any moment. She had to get him out of that cage. She also had to get the cage cleaned and get him lots more food. A dirty, hungry, locked-up Pig was something to be avoided at all costs. But that was Future Pearly's problem. Right now, Pearly the worrier had to shut down her worries – *smoky bacon to them all!* – drag herself off her shelf-bed and try to do something to save her parents.

She nibbled nervously on the muesli bar she'd found in her adventure pack. (Pig had gobbled his portion in one gulp; she really had to get him more food. Those smelly vegetable scraps were inedible.) She went over her plan in her mind again.

It wasn't much of a plan. It was basically – *GET HELP. Somehow.* Find a radio she could use – not that she knew how – or perhaps try to send an email or message on one of the computers in the common room. It was a plan way too short on details. Grandpa Woe would be very disappointed with her lack of planning. But it was all she could come up with.

Now or never. Now or Never. Pig snorted and grunted and oinked. *Now or never. Now or never.*

Pearly swallowed the mouthful of dry muesli bar she had been chewing for minutes – why didn't her parents ever put chocolate treats in their packs? Her parents...

We need you, Pearly.

GET HELP.

The words torpedoed through her brain.

Now or never! Pig banged his side against the wire of the cage. He was getting mightily agitated.

"OK!" Pearly stood up. "I'm going! I'm going. Can you smell anyone outside?"

Pig sniffed loudly. *No one – like it's been for the last two hours.*

Pearly sighed at Pig's tone and cautiously turned the door handle.

Smoky bacon to your worries, Pig encouraged. *You can do this. You are a Woe – and a clever one at that.*

Pearly poked out her tongue at him and slipped out into the hallway.

Take care, Pearly heard Pig oink, as she closed the door and started down the long echoey corridor, her heart thudding against her ribs.

The sea had calmed somewhat, which was a relief. The ship seemed to be gliding smoothly and silently, the only sounds the faint snores from the nearby cabins, and the thrum of the engines below.

Pearly tiptoed up three sets of metal stairs until she reached the deck with the common room. The air was icy. She shivered. The lights from the bridge shone brightly out across the deck, and she imagined being drawn to the bridge like a moth, with Ms Woods reaching long, spidery arms out, catching her, then wrapping her in sticky threads of web, before tossing her to a passing orca. Pearly shook the image out of her head. Smoky bacon! She had to stop this. It was not helping.

We need you, Pearly.

GET HELP.

These words pushed her along the deck to the common room, which was deserted and in darkness. The door to the bridge was closed. She'd try the computers first, she decided, mainly because she knew they were there and, well, she didn't have any other ideas.

She hoped they were switched on.

She hoped they weren't password protected.

She hoped they still had coverage this far away from Orchard Island.

Too many hopes and not enough detail – a sure sign of a hopeless plan.

Be prepared. Number 1 in the chapter about *Adventurologing: The Basics* in the *RAG. Plan. Plan. Plan.* Already this plan was a massive fail.

Well, she would have to go with Number 2: *Be prepared, but also be prepared to be spontaneous.*

Now was definitely the time for spontaneity. She didn't have anything else. She sat at one of the computer desks.

One touch of the mouse and the computer screen lit up, casting a bright blue glow into the room. Pearly gasped. She looked about desperately, half-expecting guards to appear with rifles drawn. But the room remained empty and Pearly turned her attention back to the computer.

A picture of a ship slicing through a vast sheet of ice filled the screen. A series of icons were lined up along the bottom. She hovered the cursor above each one: *Bureau of Meteorology; Tides and Swells; Icelandic News; News Today USA; The Shipping News; Finn Bay Station; Port Clementine Shipping Advisory; The World of Big Game Hunting.*

Big game hunting? That was random, but as useful as the others, which was to say, not at all. She would have to google. But whom to try first?

The police? Pearly pressed the Google icon and was relieved that no password was required. Phew.

She typed in "Orchard Island Police". The screen went white and she had to wait for ages before her search results appeared. Obviously, the internet was snail-pace slow in the middle of the ocean. She was going to have to be patient, and this was going to take way longer than she had expected. She drummed her fingers on the table in time with the throbbing of her pulse in her ears.

She scanned the results and clicked through to the Orchard Island Police website, waiting for it to materialize.

And there, right at the top under POPULAR LINKS was: REPORT A CRIME. Yes!

She clicked through to a page with a whole heap of information – too much for Pearly to read now, and most of it way beyond her anyhow. But as she scrolled down, the words ABDUCTION, ASSAULT and KIDNAPPING leaped out at her. That should cover it. It looked like she had fluked it to the right place. Her eyes flicked all over the place in a desperate search to work out how she could report Ms Woods.

Finally, there it was: the button to report a crime. She clicked it and waited while the next page loaded.

Noises drifted down from the bridge. Voices, muffled by the closed door, and also some movement. Her head pounded.

Hurry up! she urged the page, which seemed to be stuck. She refreshed and watched as words written in red gradually filled the page: *"If you are concerned for the immediate safety of yourself or another, or a crime is imminent or in progress, please call 'OOO' or your local police."*

"Smoky bacon!" she cursed under her breath in Italian. Of course she would call the police if she could, but she couldn't, and that was the point. Duh!

The rest of the page loaded to reveal a list of options to select – none of which related to her parents' situation at all. She picked one at random, and at last a page appeared with some boxes to fill in.

There were more lowered voices from behind the door to the bridge, but she couldn't stop now. This could be her one and only chance.

She started typing.

My name is Pearly Woe. I am being held captive by the famous movie star Ms Emmeline Woods on the icebreaker the Mighty Muncher *on its way to Antarctica. But that's not the problem I want to report – though it is a problem all right, and Pig and I do need rescuing – but not THE problem. The BIG problem that you need to fix first is that my parents Ricky and Angel Woe are locked in a warehouse somewhere at Port Clementine dock. Please find them. They have been there for two days already and...*

She was typing so furiously, she didn't notice the door to the bridge opening until it was too late and the hulking silhouette of Gaddi filled the space, blocking all light from behind him. Dread made Pearly's arms tingle.

"Hey!" he yelled. "What do you think you're doing?"

Pearly didn't answer. She turned back to the computer and scrolled frantically to the bottom of the page – leaving numerous boxes unfilled – until she saw the words SUBMIT. She pressed the button just as Gaddi grabbed her by the collar and wrenched her roughly out of the seat.

Gaddi held her out to one side, as if holding a skinned rabbit. He squinted at the screen. "Orchard Island Police? Are you kidding me? You are in a lot of trouble, young lady."

He hauled her out of the common room and back to Pig's cabin.

"I wouldn't want to be you when the Boss Lady finds out come morning." He slammed the door shut, and the dreaded click of the lock echoed into the night of the room.

CHAPTER 16

The door to the cabin flung open, startling Pearly so much she rolled off her sleeping shelf and landed with a thud on the floor.

Bernt stood in the doorway. "Pe-ew! It stinks worse than a walrus's fart in here." He pinched his nose and screwed up his face, making his jagged scar look red and angry, just like the rest of him.

Pig squealed indignantly. *Not my fault you make me sit in my own filth,* he oinked.

"Noisy as well as stinky," Bernt complained. "Don't know what the Boss Lady wants with you, stinky piggy, but it must be important." He wagged his finger at Pig, then turned to Pearly, who was still sprawled across the floor. "She's on her way and she's in one of her moods. Get yourself ready," he ordered.

Pearly picked herself up. She pulled down the sleeves of her jumper over her wrists. A cold draught was coming in through the open door and Pearly was reminded that they were getting closer and closer to Antarctica and further and further away from Orchard Island – and her parents.

"Where's Felix?" she asked. Her tongue felt thick and furry and her eyes itched from lack of sleep. It felt as if it was only minutes since Gaddi had tossed her into the cabin and stamped off.

"Ha! You won't be seeing that buffoon round here, girlie, not after your escapade last night, that's for sure."

Pearly chewed at her fingernails. She was worried for Felix. "Why not?" she asked, not sure she wanted the answer.

"That would be none of your business, now, wouldn't it?" Bernt said with a sneer. Bernt was definitely the Icelandic crew member she liked the least – he seemed to have a mean streak.

"The Boss Lady is going to go off like a firecracker with the stench in here."

"Can I empty my bucket in the toilet next door then?" Pearly asked, picking up the bucket and holding her breath.

Bernt snatched it from her. "I'm not falling for that one. I am not like that fool, Felix. *I* will empty it and *you* will sit here and wait for the Boss Lady." He started for the door, then twirled around. "And just in case you are thinking about doing anything silly, the Pig gets it if you're not here when I get back. Understood?"

Pearly nodded.

Bernt disappeared out the door.

Maggot, Pig oinked.

"That's an insult to maggots," Pearly replied. She perched herself on the edge of her bed-shelf. "I think Felix is in trouble, and all because of me."

Seems like it. And so are you, don't forget.

"Thanks for reminding me! Can you smell her?"

Yes. She's close. She has a unique human smell – a strong stench of cosmetics mixed with rhino blood and humanness.

Pearly tiptoed to the door and peeked out. "That's weird," she said. "There's no sign of Bernt and no Ms Woods."

She's close by, I tell you. Can't mistake that smell. Bernt is nearby too.

"Maybe all this stink is affecting your sniffer." Pearly glanced outside again. "They're not there."

She's here! She is. Pig's oinking was getting shrill. He shook himself and starting AROOing softly.

"Don't panic, Pig!"

The last time I saw that woman, she shot me. AROOO. AROOO.

"She won't shoot you – you're already in a cage."

"Just as I thought." Ms Woods's American twang filled the room. "You were communicating with the little piggy, weren't you?"

Pearly backed away from Ms Woods. "No, no I wasn't. Not in a normal way. He's getting stressed, being in that cage. I was only trying to settle him."

Ms Woods laughed. "Good try. I'd heard the rumours and I suspected it on the dinghy, but now I know it's true. I've been listening from the next room. You can communicate with the pig! This is brilliant."

"I can't!" Pearly felt the heat rise into her face. "I can't."

"Well, you had better learn how then, because if you can't, you are of no use to me or my mission ... do I make myself clear, honeybun?" Ms Woods's eyes twinkled at her through her thick eyelashes. It made Pearly want to vomit. Again.

But there was no time for that. "What have you done to my parents?" Pearly asked instead. "Where are they?"

Ms Woods laughed again. It was infuriating how hilarious she thought this all was. "Not here – as you have probably worked out. And don't go looking at me with those accusing eyes. It is not my fault. They refused my generous offer to join me. But it will be your fault if you don't ever see them again. You are the one, after all, who stowed away instead of staying on Orchard Island where you could have helped them. So I would cooperate, if I were you. Got it?"

Pearly nodded, the backs of her knees pressed up against the wire of the cage, trying to keep as much distance between her and that woman as possible.

"So listen up. This is the plan. You are coming with me on my expedition to find the Great Hairy Beast. And it will be up to you to make sure that Little Piggy uses his sniffer to locate the beast without delay." Pearly's insides twisted. There was no doubt now: Ms Woods definitely knew about Pig's power. They were in deep trouble. "And if you don't, then that's the end of Little Piggy and your parents. Any questions, honeybun?"

Two thoughts popped into Pearly's head: 1) How could calling someone "honeybun" sound so sinister? And 2) How could someone so pretty be so ugly? Wisely, she didn't voice these thoughts. She simply shook her head.

"Now clean up this filth. We have four days until we reach Finn Bay. Your job is to get the swine fit and healthy and ready for a lengthy trek in icy conditions. Gaddi and Bernt will shadow you at all times, so don't even think about pulling any stunts like last night's or it's pork chops for the pig."

Ms Woods tipped her head at Bernt and strode out of the room without another word.

Pearly's knees gave way and she sank to the floor.

"Get up and get that pig cleaned up," shouted

Bernt, unlocking the padlock to Pig's cage. "And don't try anything. I have my orders."

Pearly guided Pig out of his cage, hoping against hope that somehow her crime report to the police got through last night.

It was their only chance.

CHAPTER 17

The air was frigid up on deck, the wind howling. Pearly stood at the stern of the *Mighty Muncher* and pulled her neck warmer up over her chin, grateful that she was able to piece together some suitable, though way too big, clothes from her parents' polar gear. Stray curls whipped across her face and into her mouth. She tucked them under her woolly beanie and stared out at the open sea, the freezing wind stinging her eyes and making them water.

The vast blue ocean stretched out before her, its frothing white caps dancing in the wind. Pearly was all too aware that the ship was about to leave those white caps and the open ocean behind.

Pig huddled close beside her, his snout poking out between the deck rails, snuffling and snorting, but otherwise scarily quiet. The scar-faced Bernt puffed on a cigarette and leaned against a nearby wall out of the wind, his eyes trained on the pair constantly.

Pearly ignored Bernt's watchful gaze. She shielded her eyes and searched the skies, hoping against hope that a black speck of a helicopter would appear within the brilliant blue. She scanned the churning sea one more time for a speeding coastguard boat heading her way, coming to her rescue – before it was too late.

For the last few days, Pearly had walked the decks with Pig, getting him ready for their polar trek as Ms Woods had ordered. Gaddi or Bernt were always only a few steps behind her. It hadn't made for a comfortable walk, but it didn't stop her searching and hoping – one ear listening out for the roar of a rescue helicopter, one eye running along the horizon looking for that much-longed-for approaching boat.

But there had been nothing.

No one.

No one coming to rescue her, which probably meant that no one had rescued her parents either. Which of course meant her message hadn't got through – or if it had, the police had dismissed it as a prank.

Pearly swallowed down the bitter realization that today was probably the last day she could be rescued. The *Mighty Muncher* was about to head into the narrow channel through the pack ice, which meant they were on the edge of the Antarctic Circle and too far away to be rescued now.

The ship gave an almighty shudder. It juddered, and made a loud grinding noise.

Pig squealed. Pearly grabbed hold of the rail. Bernt flicked his cigarette overboard. They were entering the pack ice.

She headed for the bow. Pig and Bernt followed.

Pearly watched as the ship glided into the watery channel, splitting the ice in long splintering cracks and making the ship shake so much, it felt as if there was an earthquake. She looked along the side of the ship and watched as the red steel of the hull turned the white ice sheets into enormous ice cubes.

Up ahead, a huddling group of Adélie penguins scampered across the pack ice, and a lone leopard seal honked its annoyance at the mighty ship disturbing its sleep. But even these amazing sights did nothing to lift Pearly's spirits.

Pig shivered beside her. Pearly tightened the padded hood of his polar jacket, which Grandpa Woe had made him for their Alaskan holiday last year, and checked that his booties were strapped tight over his trotters. He snorted his appreciation. The Antarctic was a hostile environment – even in summer – and it was her responsibility to make sure Pig got home safely.

Home.

Would she ever see Woe Mansion again? Would she ever again jog through the apple orchard with her father? Fish in the Lemon Tree River with her mother and listen to her never-ending stories? Or work through the morning puzzles and mental challenges with Grandpa Woe?

A loud sneeze followed by a trumpeting nose blow startled Pearly out of her thoughts. Stanley Snell was harrumphing and fussing about on the small landing in front of the bridge, white breathy clouds puffing into the air around him. The Sneeze was not a healthy man. His hayfever or allergies or whatever made him so sneezy were definitely out of control.

With much clattering and bumbling, he erected his tripod and adjusted his camera, bending over, so his red snow-suited bottom stuck high into the air. The sight made Pearly giggle despite her gloomy mood. Pig spotted him too and snort-laughed.

"Hurry up!" Ms Woods climbed up the metal stairs to the landing. "I want those penguins in the shot." She was wearing an army fatigue-style snowsuit and black furry boots that reached to her knees. Her blonde waves were in a high ponytail that poked through a baseball cap. Pearly wondered how her ears weren't freezing off.

Ms Woods pulled out a small zippered bag from her snowsuit pocket, and commenced her usual routine of gazing into her hand mirror and touching up her make-up. (She wore enough make-up to plaster an entire city.) The Boss Lady and The Sneeze had been filming every day. Pearly had no idea what the filming was for. She could only guess that they were making some kind of nature documentary. But whenever she thought this, her stomach turned over, as if she had just swallowed a glass of sour milk.

Make-up fixed, Ms Woods stretched her arms out along the guardrail, leaned back against it and smiled one of her dazzling white smiles. "So we are finally here," she said into the camera. "The cracking sounds you can hear in the background are the ship breaking through the ice. After months – no, *years*," Ms Woods paused for effect, before continuing, "of careful planning and preparation..."

Pig snorted his disgust. Ms Woods stopped mid-sentence and whipped around. "You! Get out of the shot! I do not want that pig messing up the shot." She swivelled back to Stanley. "How many times do I have to tell you? Can't you get anything right?"

Stanley harrumphed and sneezed, then leaned over the rail. "Be off, you two. You are ruining our shot." He sneezed again.

"For goodness sake, Stanley, do something about that nose of yours. It's irritating the heck out of me."

Stanley blew his nose loudly in reply. "It's the cold," he snivelled. "My nose hates the cold."

"You decide to tell me this now?" Ms Woods re-did her ponytail and threaded it back through her cap. "And you, Bernt!" she yelled. "KEEP THEM AWAY FROM THE FILMING. HOW HARD CAN THAT BE?"

Pearly and Pig moved slowly away, with Pearly wondering why on earth Stanley worked for Ms Woods when she was so mean to him all the time. Bernt clomped behind them, muttering swear-words in Icelandic under his breath. Pearly glanced back to the bridge. Ms Woods was standing with her arms outstretched as if she was welcoming Antarctica, as if she owned Antarctica. She swept back to the camera and said something that Pearly couldn't hear.

It made Pearly fume. This was so against everything she had been taught about adventuring. It was all too showy. And there was something else. Something Pearly couldn't put her finger on. But with all that had happened, Pearly was sure that Ms Woods was not just making a film. No, Ms Emmeline Woods was up to no good.

CHAPTER 18

It was late afternoon by the time the *Mighty Muncher* dropped anchor in the middle of Finn Bay – though the ship's clock was the only way to know that, as the sun skirted above the horizon, never setting at this time of year. Floating islands of pack ice and jagged peaks of blue-tinged icebergs surrounded Pearly. Ahead, the shoreline marked the beginning of an endless landscape of a grey, rocky shoreline that bled into brilliant white ice as far as the eye could see. The flaming red buildings of the scientific station stood out like pimples on a bare chin. Pearly breathed in the crisp clear air, zipped her father's parka right up to her neck and pulled on her mother's huge polar gloves over her own inner gloves.

She was in Antarctica. With Pig. They were going to look for the Great Hairy Beast. This was something that her mother had dreamed about for years. This should be exciting. This should be Pearly's moment.

She should be throwing herself into the expedition for her mother's sake at the very least.

But all Pearly could think about was how she could get into that station and alert the scientists about Ms Woods and her parents' plight. Had her message got through to the police? Had her parents been found and rescued? Or were they still being held captive? These thoughts were torturing Pearly. She wiped a stray tear from her frozen cheek. Because deep down, she knew the answer. If they had been rescued, Pearly would know because she too would have been rescued by now.

Ms Woods was barking orders at the crew as they loaded up an inflatable Zodiac with supplies. The scar-faced Bernt was leaning against the rail, guarding Pearly and Pig. Pearly could feel his mean eyes watching her every move. Gaddi was helping to swing a large crate hanging from the ship's crane onto the Zodiac. Felix was nowhere in sight. Still. Pearly hadn't spotted him since the day he left her door unlocked, and she feared for his safety.

She was cursed, she was sure of it. Everything she touched turned to disaster.

Ms Woods swung around to face her and Pig.

"OK, honeybun. In you go!" she called out to Pearly. "And make sure that swine doesn't end up overboard. Frozen bacon won't help me find the beast, now, will it?" Her tone was honey but her words were

109

lemon sour. Pearly thought that she would probably never be able to eat honey again, without thinking of lemons.

Pearly helped Pig onto the canvas swing that was going to lower them onto the Zodiac. It rocked and lurched out over the deep blue sea, then with a creaking jolt began its descent. Ms Woods had clambered down the ladder and stood at the back of the Zodiac, tiller in her hand ready. Stanley Snell was crouched beside her, huffing and puffing, like an anxious dragon, his cheeks flushed from the cold. He snapped a few close-up shots, then changed to his video camera and panned across the bay.

"Hurry up!" Ms Woods yelled as Pearly and Pig squeezed onoard up towards the front. Pig perched himself on top of a stack of plastic crates and Pearly found a spot pressed up against a damp canvas sheet covering a large, mysterious object that dug into her sides.

It wasn't until the Zodiac sped away from the *Mighty Muncher* that Pearly realized they were alone with Ms Woods and Stanley. The rest of the crew had stayed on board. Not even Bernt or Gaddi had come with them.

Expect the unexpected, the *RAG* said.

This was certainly unexpected, and not in a good way. Alone with the Boss Lady and her sniffy, sneezy photographer who was allergic to the cold. The thought made Pearly's guts gurgle.

It also made her wonder, not for the first time, about Ms Woods's motives. Pearly knew that she kidnapped Pig because of his special tracking power. But why lock up her parents? Ms Woods had made a point of blaming Pearly for her parents' situation, but she hadn't seemed bothered by the fact that they were still locked up. That was extreme. Surely making a nature documentary or whatever she was doing wasn't worth kidnapping a pig and risking harm to her parents? Why was she so intent on finding the Great Hairy Beast anyway? What would a famous movie star want with the Great Hairy Beast? And if she wasn't a famous movie star, then what was she famous for? Pearly had started to suspect that she might be one of those noisy fame-seeking TV adventurers – the type the Guild loathed. The type that made a fuss about their adventures and often left a trail of destruction in their wake. This was not a good thought. But even the showiest TV adventurer didn't resort to crime for their shows ... did they?

The *RAG*'s charter was all about doing things quietly, about never disturbing the balance. Respect. Care. The beast had fascinated Pearly's mother for as long as Pearly could remember. She had been on two expeditions to try to find it. But she had only wanted to prove that it existed. It was a scientific challenge for her, the ultimate goal, given her fascination with rare beasts. Somehow, Pearly didn't think that Ms Woods held the same noble intentions. The thought made her chest fill with an aching sadness that was mingling uncomfortably with a horrible bubbling anger.

The Zodiac bumped along between the ice floes. It was not an easy ride.

Pearly set her eyes on the red buildings of the scientific station. They were her only chance. She had to come up with a plan to get inside. A better plan than her last one: *GET HELP. Somehow.* But, sadly, that was all she had so far.

She was going to have to wing it and *be prepared to be spontaneous* again – even though her last attempt at spontaneity had disastrous results.

They drew closer to the curve in the bay near the scientific station, and hopes of being able to alert the authorities began to rise up in Pearly.

But her hopes vaporized in a second.

Instead of heading for the red buildings, Ms Woods took a sharp turn to the left that made Pearly gasp and Pig squeal.

"Where are we going?" yelled Pearly, over the roar of the outboard motor, clutching her adventure pack to her chest.

Ms Woods revved the engine in reply and sent the Zodiac flying across the inky water, swerving right then left, avoiding large lumps of ice in her way. Seals dived off icebergs in fright. Penguins scattered. Terns and petrels took to the air.

"Hold tight, Pig!" Pearly shouted uselessly. Because, frankly, how was Pig meant to hold on when he was perched on top of plastic crates and only had booted trotters to hold on with? He slid perilously from side to side as if skating on ice, nearly tumbling off a number of times before being sent sliding back in the opposite direction. By the time the Zodiac raced up onto a rocky shore well out of sight of Finn Bay Station, Pig was not a happy pig. And Pearly was furious.

"What was that about?" Pearly bounded out of the boat and tossed her pack onto the shore. "I thought you said you didn't want frozen bacon?"

"Hurry up," Ms Woods said, her chin held high in a pose for Stanley. "Get this stuff off."

"You almost sent Pig into that freezing water!" Pearly persisted. "His sniffer would be no use then."

Ms Woods fluttered her eyelashes at Pearly in a way that made Pearly want to slug her. "Did he fall off, honey?"

"No," said Pearly.

"So what are you banging on about then? Make yourself useful and get those crates unloaded. We have no time to waste."

Anger (and possibly the freezing temperature) froze Pearly to the spot. Ms Woods was a poor excuse for a human being, that was for sure! And now Pearly's last chance to alert the authorities had been taken away from her. Why were they here, in this spot? Why didn't Ms Woods check in with the station? Even Pearly knew that this was expected. It might even be a law. You couldn't just rock up on Antarctica and go on a camping trip. Pig had clambered off and had his snout to the ground, sniffing.

Trouble, he oinked. *I smell trouble. Lots of it.* He sounded unusually panicked.

Me too, thought Pearly, as a loud throaty roar filled the icy air.

Pearly spun around. A shiny orange skidoo with Ms Woods on board puttered off the Zodiac ramp and onto the shore. Stanley stood a few paces back, his video camera rolling.

"Hook up the trailer and load her up!" said Ms Woods. "Move it, honeybun! This isn't a *pig*nic, you know." Ms Woods laughed so hard at her own joke that her hood fell off, and she grabbed Stanley's arm to steady herself. "*Pig*nic – ha-ha! *Pig*nic!"

Stanley sneezed in reply.

Pearly looked at Pig. Pig looked at Pearly.

This was definitely no *pig*nic.

This was a lot of *hog*wash!

CHAPTER 19

Pearly and Pig were squeezed into a tight space at the back of the over-full trailer behind the skidoo. Pearly didn't mind. She liked the distance from Ms Woods and Stanley with his sneezes and snuffles. Besides, being close to Pig meant she could feel the warmth of his hide through his polar jacket and the evenness of his breathing, and that was comforting.

The skidoo was slow and bumpy as it travelled over the rocky shoreline. So bumpy that Pearly's head felt as if it might shake right off her shoulders. But once on the ice field it zipped along at a furious pace, shards of ice flying past Pearly's ears. It was jolly freezing, which was bad for her, but good for Pig. He was not good in the heat. Pig held his snout out into the frozen air and let the wind caress his ears. Occasionally he gave a little worried squeal.

Pearly shared his worry. Of course. It was her nature, after all, to worry. And now she had more to worry about than ever before. She knew that travelling across Antarctica in search of the Great Hairy Beast should be a thrilling experience. This was an Adventurologist-in-Training's dream mission, and her mother's greatest wish. But with her parents in trouble and Pig's safety in her hands, it was far from thrilling or dream-like for Pearly.

Her last chance of helping her parents had vanished, and that filled Pearly's heart with a great ugly lump of despair. And the worrisome thoughts about Ms Woods and her motives certainly weren't helping.

What was in it for Ms Woods? This question continued to batter Pearly. She tried to *think outside the box,* like the *RAG* suggested, to come at the problem from every angle, but that didn't seem to help. She recalled how the *RAG* stated that *logic was your friend.* There was nothing logical about Ms Woods, but logic told Pearly that the awful woman definitely wasn't a scientist. There was nothing scientific about her. She was all about sounding sweet, looking good and posing for the camera. Which fitted with her being a famous film star, but not really a nature documentary maker. She certainly wasn't an explorer, and if she was an adventurer she was the worst kind.

And then there was Stanley. Was he in on "it" – whatever "it" was? Pearly suspected not. He seemed to be nothing more than a hired hand who did as he was told. But she couldn't be sure. After all, she knew to *expect the unexpected.*

Oh, it was all so confounding!

But there was no denying that there was more to this expedition than finding the beast and making a documentary or some kind of film about it. Pearly was convinced there was something decidedly sinister about Ms Woods and her quest.

On and on they zoomed, Pearly and Pig being jolted from side to side as the skidoo traversed the rough landscape.

Deeper and deeper into a frozen white world they went.

Further and further from the scientists at Finn Bay Station.

Further and further from any hope of Pearly doing something to help her parents.

They zipped along beside a mighty jagged glacier, over one enormous ice field to another. They negotiated their way through steep gullies of ice. They skirted around rocky ridges, their craggy peaks poking out from the ice.

Pearly wished she knew where they were headed. Ms Woods had been tight-lipped whenever Pearly had asked, which only made Pearly all the more suspicious. They were a long way from shore and the *Mighty Muncher*. There wasn't a penguin, gull or seal in sight. Only kilometres and kilometres and kilometres of ice.

At last they came to a sudden stop.

Pizza break? oinked Pig hopefully.

Ms Woods cut the engine and stomped around to the back of the trailer. "Get that pig off his porky behind," she said, and laughed. Pearly was not impressed with Ms Woods's new sense of humour. What had turned her into a comedian all of a sudden? She was becoming pretty obnoxious, her eyes gleeful and hungry behind her red goggles. "And tell him to put that sniffer to work, while the skies are still clear and the light good."

"Come on, Pig," Pearly said, gazing up at the enormous cliffs of ice and rocky ridges before them. "Best do what Ms Woods says."

Ms Woods pushed her goggles up over her beanie and then pulled a folded map and compass from her rucksack. She opened the map and held it out for Stanley to see. Stanley stood behind her, his many chins straining as he looked over her shoulder. Ms Woods pursed her red lips as she studied the map. She turned around slowly, checking her map and compass constantly, Stanley shuffling around with her. "Yep. This looks right," she said.

"Shall we take a few shots with that jagged peak in view, Emmeline?" Stanley asked. "The charcoal grey will make your snowsuit pop beautifully."

"Sure. But keep the kid and the pig out of sight." Ms Woods shoved the map back into her rucksack, smoothed her wavy hair around her face and ran her tongue over her teeth. She put one leg on the step of the skidoo and thrust her chin in the air. Stanley snapped away.

Pearly shook her head. This was the weirdest expedition in the history of expeditions. She glanced over at the map sticking out of the rucksack, and sidled towards it. *Information is power.* Grandpa Woe's words came to her. She needed information. She needed that map.

But as her gloved fingers gripped the edge of the map, Ms Woods lurched at her and snatched it away.

"You really can't be trusted, can you now?" she twanged. "Stanley, you need to keep better watch!"

"It would help if you told us something, you know," Pearly tried, feeling exasperated. "Why do you think the Great Hairy Beast is here? What should we be looking for?"

Ms Woods pulled out her make-up bag and reapplied her lipstick as she considered this. She snapped her hand mirror shut and slipped her make-up bag back into her pocket. "OK then. It's probably time," she said. She opened the map again. "The Great Hairy Beast has been sighted only a handful of times over the past decade. Here, here and a few times over here." She stabbed her gloved finger at the map awkwardly. Pearly knew all this of course – it was her mother's pet subject – but she remained mute. "But in the last couple of weeks there have been two sightings directly west of Finn Bay near Mount Gamble – here." She pointed to the jagged mountain peak pushing out of the ice to the right of them. "Plus this!"

Ms Woods thrust the map under her arm, before retrieving her mobile phone from the inside pocket of her jacket. She opened an app on her phone and produced a bundle of photos of white icy ground.

Pearly's heart started to gallop. She looked at the photos and tried to show interest. But that phone was screaming at her like an alarm. Would it work here in Antarctica? Could she get a message to the police or the station or someone? Could she help her parents after all?

Pig sensed her unease and grunted beside her.

"See," hissed Ms Woods. Pearly couldn't see anything except whitish snow. "Look closely!"

"Bear prints?" Pearly took the phone with trembling hands and held the photo out so Pig could see too. "There are no bears in Antarctica," she said, wondering what would happen if she made a run for it with the phone. She lifted her eyes up and scanned her surroundings. The skidoo. Perhaps she could steal it?

"Precisely," said Ms Woods, breaking into her thoughts. "And these are not bear prints. These are the paw prints of the Great Hairy Beast."

Pearly examined the huge paw prints pressed into the ice: the enormous kidney-shaped paw, the five long toes, the sharp scratches of dagger-like claws. The sight made her shiver.

How does she know these are from the Great Hairy Beast? oinked Pig.

"My thoughts exactly," Pearly said to Pig, then she turned to Ms Woods. "Why the Great Hairy Beast?"

Ms Woods tapped the side of her head. "Deduction," she said. "And cleverness." Stanley harrumphed at that, and Pearly had to swallow a giggle. "Scientists from Finn Bay Station sighted the Great Hairy Beast on the same day as they came across these prints. There are no animals in Antarctica that can make these prints – it can only be the Great Hairy Beast!"

Pearly had to admit it made sense, and even as her mind was whirring wildly, desperately trying to work out a way to steal the phone and make her escape, she was starting to catch Ms Woods's enthusiasm.

"That's why I need the pig," said Ms Woods, her excited gleam replaced with a hungry glint – the type of glint one might get when imagining a plate piled with crispy bacon or sticky pork ribs, which was a disturbing thought on many levels. "Others have tried and failed.

Emmeline Woods does not fail, do you hear me? His sniffer is my secret weapon. I hope you have it in good working order."

Pig AROOOed. Pearly tensed. She knew Pig didn't like being spoken about like this. It made him feel like an object, rather than a living breathing lovable pig. Besides, his snout wasn't a car engine that could be tuned and maintained. And it certainly wasn't a weapon. That word sent alarm racing through Pearly.

She rubbed her gloved hand along Pig's back to try to calm him. "It's working perfectly," Pearly said. "He's been able to smell you from one end of the ship to the other. You have a strong meaty scent, you know."

Pearly's face felt hot. She didn't know where those words came from – they just jumped out of her mouth of their own accord.

OINKY SQUEALIO-O, whispered Pig, which was pig for, *You're terrible, Pearly.*

Stanley sniggered quietly, pretending to polish his camera lens.

Ms Woods's own mouth flopped open with shock. "But can it sniff out the Great Hairy Beast, honeybun?" she demanded, snatching the phone from Pearly's grip.

Ah, smoky bacon! Her eyes zeroed in on Ms Woods's phone, following it as Ms Woods started packing things into her rucksack. "Ah, um, I'm sure he will be able to detect its presence," she said.

I'm detecting the presence of a dirty rat right now, oinked Pig.

"What did he say?" twanged Ms Woods, gazing at Pig with suspicious eyes.

"He said that he is up for the challenge." Pearly watched Ms Woods as she flicked through some images on her phone. Could she grab it and run?

"OK, get crackling then. Let the sniffing begin." Ms Woods laughed loudly and slapped Stanley on the back. Stanley pretended to laugh too, then stepped away to give his nose a trumpeting blow in his handkerchief. Ms Woods poked the map and compass back into her rucksack, then slipped the phone back into the inside pocket of her snow jacket and pulled up the zip.

Pearly's stomach dropped. She had missed her chance.

Again.

CHAPTER 20

They plodded across the ice for what seemed like hours. The sun was low in the sky, pale and weak through thin ribbons of cloud. Ms Woods had them walking in circles around the skidoo, moving further away with each circle. Stanley clicked and snapped and harrumphed. His breath was coming in short gasps and he stopped constantly to mop his face. Pearly worried how he was going to survive in this freezing environment.

Pig had his snout to the ground. He sniffled and snuffled and oinked and grunted, his curly tail wagging in the frigid air.

"What's he saying?" Ms Woods asked continually. "What can he smell?"

"Nothing unusual. Some birds. And a seal, that's it," replied Pearly. But there was no way she was going to let Ms Woods know even if Pig did smell something. Not while she wasn't sure of the woman's motives.

The skidoo was barely visible – just an orange speck in the distant white – when Pig confessed that his sniffer was getting pretty frozen and he wasn't sure how long it would work in these conditions.

Pearly scratched his back in sympathy. "Pig's getting cold," Pearly called to Ms Woods, who was a few metres ahead. "Can we set up camp now?"

Ms Woods let out a wild shriek. She swung around and danced a little jig, her arms above her head, hands clasped in a victory salute.

That was not the reaction Pearly was expecting.

OINKY OINKY NO-NO! oinked Pig.

"Tracks!" Ms Woods shouted. "Tracks!"

Pearly and Pig bounded up, slipping and sliding, to where Ms Woods was doing her awkward dance, and where Stanley stood scratching his beanied head and harrumphing. And there, sure enough, stamped into the ice were the enormous tracks of what was certain to be the Great Hairy Beast.

The paw prints were massive, that's for sure. But there were only about a dozen of them leading into a deep drift of snow alongside the peak of Mount Gamble. Then they disappeared.

Pig's snout frantically whipped back and forth, back and forth across the ice, trying to get a scent. He was grunting and oinking, his curly tail straightening in frustration.

"What's going on? Can he smell it?" asked Ms Woods.

Pearly shrugged, as the three followed close behind Pig.

Strange. Very strange, Pig oinked to Pearly. *I can smell bear. But I can also smell human – and not the Boss Lady or The Sneeze either. Different human. Most baffling.*

That was indeed baffling, and Pearly wasn't sure what she was going to tell Ms Woods, who was scowling at Pig. "What is it? I demand to know."

"Well ... it's a little mysterious actually..." Pearly started carefully, her eyes scanning the icy landscape around her. Human? There was a human here? How was that possible? "He can smell, um, er, human. Not us. Someone else."

"Preposterous. I think that sniffer is a dud. Tell him to try harder. I simply won't have it. And you better not be telling me porkies."

Stanley laughed automatically.

Pearly tensed.

Pig groaned. He AROOed softly under his breath, then put his snout to the ice and continued sniffing.

Still bear – polar bear, I think – with a side whiff of human, Pig told Pearly. *And it's definitely not you or her or him. Someone else. But definitely two scents.*

"Tell me what he's saying!" Ms Woods was losing her patience fast. "And stop filming, Stanley. I said no shots with the pig."

126

"He thinks you're right. His sniffer is playing up. It's too cold. Perhaps we should try again tomorrow?" Pearly tried, a growing sense of unease making her voice quaver. Bear and human – that was scary, as well as weird.

Ms Woods chewed on her bottom lip, considering. Pearly held her breath.

"I am rather famished, Emmeline," said Stanley. "And a tad weary..." He sneezed for effect.

"Oh, all right then. None of you have any stamina!" Ms Woods said finally. "But that pig's snout better work properly tomorrow – or I won't be needing you two any longer, will I, honeybun?"

Pearly tried to smile.

OINKY OINKY NO-NO! oinked Pig.

CHAPTER 21

Pearly lay awake in her little dome tent. The sleeping bag was thick and snug and she was surprisingly warm – especially with Pig squashed up against her.

Outside was so still and quiet, it was creepy. A pale midnight sun hung above the horizon, casting long thin shadows across the ice. It was hard to get your head around – the sun never setting. It only made Pearly feel all the more out of her depth, and so very tiny and insignificant within this huge white never-ending world.

Alone. Afraid. And anxious.

So many fears were pressing against her skull, it felt as though it might explode. She imagined a devilish creature, half-bear, half-human, skulking about outside. She imagined Ms Woods working out that she wasn't telling the truth about what Pig could smell, and zooming off on the skidoo with The Sneeze, leaving her and Pig alone in the middle of Antarctica. But more than anything, she imagined that phone –

that phone being almost in Pearly's grasp and then it hurtling up into the sky and smashing against a rocky mound. That phone – her last chance to get help for her parents – in a thousand useless pieces tumbling across a jagged glacier.

Are you going to at least try? Pig oinked softly.

"How?" Pearly whispered back.

Pig sighed, a long snorty sigh. *I don't know. I could make a racket and run off and then you could grab the phone while she chases me.*

Pearly appreciated Pig's offer, but it was too dangerous. "She shot you once before. We can't risk it."

Pearly wiggled out of her sleeping bag, unzipped the door and stuck her head outside. The tips of her ears froze in the frigid air. Not surprisingly, Stanley was a snorer and his tent rumbled like an approaching storm. There was no movement from Ms Woods's tent. She was probably asleep too, and the phone was with her inside that tent, still in her jacket pocket. Pearly looked across to the skidoo. Should they try to escape? Her *amma* had a similar machine that she let Pearly drive last summer in Iceland. The skidoo would operate in a similar way, surely...

It was worth a try. She pulled on her parka, rolled up the overlong sleeves and tugged on her beanie and boots. "Stay here," she told Pig. "I'm going to take a look at the skidoo."

Pig squealed with worry, and scrambled to the open flap of the tent. *Be careful!*

It was freezing outside – colder even than Iceland. Pearly wished it were dark though. She had no cover. She took a calming breath, then crept towards the machine. The crunch of her boots on the ice sounded like an advancing army in the silence of the low sun, despite her efforts to walk quietly. Ms Woods was bound to hear her.

As she slowly approached the skidoo, a shiver ran right through her, and she was consumed by the overwhelming feeling that she was being watched. She looked about her. Nothing. No one. Only ice and snow and long blue shadows. And really, how could there be someone watching?

The skidoo's trailer still had most of their supplies on board, with the exception of their camping gear and a glossy black case that Ms Woods had ordered a harrumphing Stanley to put in her tent – and "be sure not to drop it!" Pearly checked the console for a starter button. There wasn't one. Only a key ignition. *Mamma mia!* And of course, there was no key – that must be with Ms Woods too.

Pearly licked her lips and looked towards Ms Woods's tent – everything she needed was in there. In there with the *famous* Ms Emmeline Woods! It was another hopeless situation. Grandpa Woe and the

Adventurologists' Guild should add a chapter about what to do in Hopeless Situations. Or perhaps Hopeless Situations only happened to failed Adventurologists.

She took a tentative step back towards her tent, just as Ms Woods's tent flap flew open. Ms Woods stumbled out onto the ice, pulling on her parka and shoving a beanie over her tangle of hair.

"What do you think you're doing?" she growled, rubbing at her eyes, which were rimmed with smudged mascara.

"I need to go to the loo," Pearly said, without missing a beat.

"Not near our supplies! Go over behind the tents. And hurry up. I want to make an early start tomorrow."

Pearly tramped behind the tent, feeling Ms Woods's eyes upon her.

That went well. Not!

Pearly woke the next morning with an unusual feeling.

At first she couldn't quite work it out. She felt different. Fierce. Determined. As if nothing or no one was going to stop her today. It was a peculiar feeling – like eating too many hotdogs, knowing that you're going to end up feeling sick, but happily stuffing more into your mouth regardless. It made her rather dizzy.

Maybe it's the hopelessness of the situation, she reasoned. *Perhaps this is how it feels when what is real is worse than what you can imagine. Or maybe it's just that never-ending sun making me feel odd and messing with my brain.*

But whatever it was, she felt different. After settling back into her tent last night, she had lain there in the glow of the night-time sun thinking, while Pig gently snored. She mentally flipped through the pages of the *RAG*, wishing again she'd had the foresight to pack it into her adventure pack before leaving Woe Mansion.

Two guidelines in particular, from the chapter *Adventurologing: The Basics*, were demanding her attention.

Number 3: Know your limits. She had always found this, well, *limiting* – mainly because she had so many limitations! Her only strength was her language ability, and that was causing her no end of trouble.

But Number 3 was paired with Number 4, and it was Number 4 that seemed to be making this fierce determination bloom.

Number 4: Push your limits.

This is what she had to do. She had to push past all her worries about what *might* happen and just get the job done. Smoky bacon to her worries, like Pig always said. It was that simple. It had always been that simple.

But today, it also *felt* that simple. And the job at hand was to GET THAT PHONE! Or the keys to the skidoo – or both. She felt as free as the giant petrels soaring over the glaciers.

Pig was not so enthusiastic, however, and had spent the morning reminding Pearly about Ms Woods's threats and the fact that they were in the middle of Antarctica.

But Pearly would not be deterred.

While Pig gobbled his breakfast of dried oats, Pearly started pulling down their tent. She kept one eye on Stanley and the other on Ms Woods – waiting for her moment.

Stanley had already packed everything up, and was now slumped against a rock eating his breakfast. He jiggled around impatiently as he chewed, *harrumphing* every now and then. It made Pearly chuckle softly to herself.

Pearly trained her attention on Ms Woods. Her tent was packed up and waiting to be loaded onto the skidoo. So was that black glossy case. *What was in it?* Pearly wondered. It was obviously valuable or important. Ms Woods was leaning against the skidoo, squinting into her small hand mirror and applying her layers of make-up. Pearly watched as she painted on her lipstick, smacked her lips at the mirror, then set to work coaxing her waves of hair into a long ponytail.

Once that was done, she slid her phone from the furry side pocket of her red parka.

Pearly's breath caught in her throat and she tripped over a tent rope.

"Be careful there," Ms Woods called out without looking up from her phone. "Break that and you sleep on the snow." Ms Woods held out the phone, turning her head from side to side, trying to get the perfect angle for a selfie.

That phone was screaming at Pearly.

"What are you gawking at now?" Ms Woods twanged at Pearly as she plugged the phone into a power pack and then perched it on top of her rucksack. "Hurry up! Have you even eaten, and all? And the pig? Hey there, where is the pig?"

Pearly snapped her head around. Pig was nowhere in sight. She tried not to smile. That Pig – he had grumbled about how risky her plan was, but here he was creating a decoy. Pearly loved him for it.

"I ... I ... don't know," Pearly said truthfully, adding a little worry to her voice. *"Mamma mia! Questo è terribile!"* she broke out in Italian.

"Speak English! And find that pig!"

Pearly started off at a run.

"NO!" shouted Ms Woods. "Come back here. I'm not having you running off like that. I'm no fool. You call out to him. We'll go look for him. Stan-*ley*! The pig.

The pig's gone. Go look along that track!" Ms Woods ordered, before striding off in the direction of Mount Gamble.

Stanley harrumphed. He slid off the rock and tramped off, following the ruts made by the skidoo. "Piggy!" he called. "Little piggy. Come back here…"

Pearly headed straight for the skidoo, her eyes on that phone. "Pi-ig!" she pretend-called. "Pi-ig! Where are you?"

As soon as she reached the skidoo, she grabbed the phone.

Luckily it was unlocked.

She searched the screen to see if there was coverage, and her heart plummeted to her toes. The bars across the top were empty. No coverage.

Pearly went to toss the phone back into the rucksack and look for the keys to the skidoo, when the photo on the screensaver grabbed her attention. Her legs became wobbly. Her breath wedged in her throat.

It was a photo of Ms Emmeline Woods being all famous – posing on the cover of a magazine – *BIG GAME* magazine. A rifle was slung over her shoulder and an enormous dead rhinoceros lay beside her.

Smoky bacon!

Ms Woods was a big game hunter!

Of course she was.

She was famous, all right.

Famous for killing animals.

Pearly opened the photo app and flicked through Ms Woods's albums. There was photo after photo of Ms Woods with dead animals – lions, bears, giraffes, hippos, moose. It seemed as though she had her own TV hunting show. Pearly scrolled and found pictures of Ms Woods's house, which was filled with more stuffed animals than Pearly could bear to identify. It made her nauseous. Then she found a photo of another magazine article with the headline: *Emmeline Woods has conquered the BIG FIVE. What's next for the world's number one game hunter?*

What's next?

Pearly knew the answer.

The Great Hairy Beast of Antarctica, that's what.

CHAPTER 22

Pig appeared not long after Pearly had made her gruesome discovery. He had his snout to the ice and was oinking softly, OINKY OINKY NO-NO! OINKY OINKY NO-NO!

"Trouble, all right," said Pearly, as she showed Pig a few of the images. "That's why she's here. That's why she wants *you*. The Great Hairy Beast is going to be her next kill. And she wants you to track it."

Pig snorted. He kicked his legs out behind him.

A tear slid down Pearly's cheek. "This will destroy Mum."

We won't let it happen, Pig oinked. *Find the key.*

"Agreed," said Pearly. "We need to get out of here." She tossed the phone onto the crate and started rummaging through Ms Woods's rucksack for the key to the skidoo.

Then it struck her. She stopped. She dropped the rucksack and plopped to the ice.

"We can't go," she said through her sniffles, her eyes moving to that shiny black case. She suddenly had an idea of what it might contain. "If we go and she finds the beast, it will be dead for sure. If we stay, we might be able to send her off in the wrong direction. We can throw her off the scent. Pig, we are the Great Hairy Beast's only chance."

But what about your parents? Pig snuggled his snout into Pearly's lap and made soft crooning piggy noises. *If we don't get help soon ... it could be too late.*

Pearly nodded grimly, her chin to her chest, trying to choke back the sobs that were threatening to erupt. It was an impossible choice.

Her fierce determination of only a few minutes ago had evaporated. Now she was a puddle of worries once more. She didn't know what to do.

"What are you blubbing about?" Ms Woods's voice startled Pearly to her feet.

"I ... er ... I'm just relieved that I found Pig." Pearly wiped her cheeks with her sleeve. It looked as if her decision was made for her. No way could she steal the skidoo with Ms Woods around.

Ms Woods narrowed her eyes at Pig. "And where was he?"

"I ... I ... don't know," Pearly said. "He just appeared." Pig sat at Pearly's feet and put his head on his front trotters.

"Well, ask him."

"I did. He won't tell me. He can be stubborn sometimes."

"You better not be up to something, honeybun." Ms Woods cupped her hands over her mouth and called for Stanley to come back.

"Hurry up. Put your gear on the skidoo. We're moving our base to the other side of Mount Gamble. We'll start again from there."

Minutes later they were all goggled and gloved and zipped up tight, on the skidoo and on their way.

Dread prickled right through Pearly. She felt more than ever that she was deserting her parents, but she knew she needed to save the Great Hairy Beast from Ms Woods.

And she couldn't do both.

Ms Woods stopped the skidoo beside two tall icy columns that looked like giant icicles bursting up to the sky. She grabbed her rucksack, shoved in her map and compass and some food parcels, reapplied her lipstick and then ordered Stanley to take a few shots.

Pearly checked her own pack and added in some muesli and protein bars and extra water for Pig.

"This way," ordered Ms Woods. "Pig – in front."

Pearly swung around to see Ms Woods taking a

high-powered rifle with a telescopic scope out of the large black case.

Pearly gasped. Her hunch was spot-on.

"For protection," Ms Woods said, and Stanley laughed. Ms Woods glared at him. She arranged her ponytail down one shoulder, and then slung her rifle over the other. "Hurry up, y'all! And no nonsense."

Pig snorted. He trotted past Ms Woods, flicking snow into her face.

Sorry, he grunted, then added, *not*, and snort-laughed as he put his snout to the ice and got sniffing.

Snow coated Ms Woods's goggles and she scowled at Pearly as if it was her fault.

Pearly shrugged, tucked the overlong legs of her snow trousers into her boots and walked on to catch up with Pig. Stanley followed, holding his camera in front of him and sniffling and puffing and giggling. Pearly had no idea what was so funny.

They took a route around the mountain beside a wide glacier. The ice was as slippery as a banana skin bathed in olive oil. Stanley slipped over every other step, *harrumphing* and cursing, his face flushed, his chins glistening with sweat.

The ice here was too smooth and hard for paw prints, so Ms Woods diverted them towards the soft patches of snow along the edges of a rocky outcrop.

But there were no paw prints there either.

Ms Woods was getting grumpier by the second, especially as Pearly kept on telling her that Pig was picking up no new scents.

Which was a lie, of course.

The twin scents of polar bear and human were still there – the bear scent was diminishing, but the human scent was getting stronger. And this was so baffling that it made Pearly's face hot and sweaty, despite the freezing temperatures. Somehow, they were going to have to get Ms Woods to turn back. Or they might stumble right into the path of whatever the strange scents belonged to.

"Anything?" Ms Woods asked, yet again.

"Not a thing," replied Pearly.

"A dud sniffer," she grumbled. "That's what I think is the problem here."

An animal murderer, oinked Pig. *That's what I think is the problem here.*

"What did he say?" demanded Ms Woods.

"Still nothing, except us."

As Pearly lumbered across the ice to catch up with Pig, she caught sight of something out of the corner of her eye. She flicked her head around and examined the lumpy ice and scattered rocks nearby. There was nothing there.

Pig grunted and shoved his snout in and around some clumps of ice and rock.

"Did you see that?" Pearly whispered.

What?

"I swear I saw something move – over there, by those rocks."

Think you are imagining things again, though I am getting an increasing scent of human. And it's not the animal murderer or the sneezy photographer.

Pearly's arms prickled. What did that mean? Is that what she just saw? A person? She didn't get a good look, but it seemed too small to be the beast. She couldn't ask Pig though, without Ms Woods overhearing them.

Finally, Ms Woods signalled for them to stop for lunch. Pearly sat on the top of a boulder jutting out of the snow. It was as far away from Ms Woods and Stanley as Ms Woods would allow. She nibbled her protein bar and listened to Ms Woods instructing Stanley on the post-lunch filming. Pearly hoped she could talk to Pig then. Ms Woods didn't like them anywhere near her when she was filming.

She gnawed at the edges of the tasteless bar. It was so frozen that she could only scrape off the tiniest of pieces. Pig lay beside her and hoed into more oats. He was not impressed with the menu.

They were packing up from lunch, and Pearly was looking for her chance to speak to Pig, when things changed.

And not in a good way.

The first sign of trouble was a large and towering bank of clouds appearing on the horizon. Within seconds of noticing the clouds, an almighty gale came rushing over Mount Gamble. It knocked Pearly off her feet and onto her backside and sent Pig skating across the ice on his booted trotters. Ms Woods bowed her head into the windstorm, planting her feet firmly in a snowdrift. Stanley crouched low, his body bent double, protecting his precious camera.

With the wind came the clouds. And with the clouds, a blizzard. And soon snow was blasting Pearly so fiercely, it felt as if she was being hit by nails. The temperature plummeted. She could barely stay upright. She couldn't even see her glove as she held it up in front of her face. It was a total white-out. Images of being swept away by the wind and sent swirling into the depths of the snowy continent raced through her mind. Pig bowed his snout into the wind and planted his trotters into the snow. Stanley was swiftly turning into an instant snowman.

"What do we do?" Pearly yelled, her voice barely audible over the roar of the wind. "Should we pitch camp and wait it out?"

"Are you stupid?" Ms Woods yelled back. "We have to keep moving. It's so cold now, if we stop, we'll freeze to death! That's if we don't get buried alive first."

Pig squealed with fright.

Frozen to death? Buried alive? These were not options. Once again, these were even worse than Pearly's imaginings. "But we can't see!" shouted Pearly. "We'll lose each other."

Ms Woods looked about helplessly. Stanley was having a frenzied sneezing fit. Pearly sensed panic was setting into the pair of them. And that was not good.

The snow was already building around them – soon they would all be snowmen. She had to do something.

And that was when the *RAG* came to mind – her brain opening it up to the pages about Surviving Sticky Situations again and *taking initiative* and *thinking outside the box* and *keeping your wits about you*. Her mind was a hurricane of worries, but she willed them away – *smoky bacon to you all!* – and searched for the wonderful resolve she had felt only that morning. Which immediately made her think of Grandpa Woe and her parents who always seemed to be in control and know what to do. What would they do in a situation like this?

A situation like this!

That was it.

The foggy highlands of Scotland.

Last year her parents had been in a situation exactly like this. The weather had closed in on a trek across the Scottish highlands and they couldn't see a thing. One wrong step could have seen them hurtling over a cliff. She remembered her father saying they had to keep their wits about them and take initiative in order to get themselves out of this dangerously sticky situation.

It was time for Pearly to take the initiative!

It was time for rope.

She wrenched her adventure pack off her shoulder and rummaged inside, pulling out three lengths of rope.

"What use is that?" shouted Ms Woods. "What are you going to do – tie yourselves to a lump of ice? Frozen bacon in an hour."

Pearly didn't answer. She tied two lengths of rope to the belt holding her snow trousers up, then tied the other end of one length to a toggle on the hood of Pig's jacket and handed the end of the other length to Stanley. "Here, tie this to your belt. And then use this one to tie yourself to Ms Woods. That way we can keep walking and we won't lose each other. My parents did this last year in Scotland."

Stanley harrumphed. Ms Woods scowled, but Pearly could tell she knew it was a good idea. Ms Woods reached her hand out through the raging storm, grabbed the rope from Stanley and fastened it to the belt of her parka.

They pulled on their balaclavas, snow goggles, extra thick beanies and any other stick of clothing they could find. And off they plodded, Ms Woods leading the way.

The wind shrieked at Pearly. The snow blasted her. Charming little icicles hung from the tip of her nose.

But on and on and on the four trudged through the driving snow.

Walking blind. Stumbling. Tripping. Falling over. But keeping together.

And, right on cue, Pearly's worries returned.

She worried that she might fall down a crevice or step off a cliff. She worried that Pig might get buried in the snow. She worried that his pink hide wasn't thick enough to keep him warm, even with his polar jacket.

She was worrying so much that she stepped into an extra deep snowdrift, the snow coming right up to the top of her thigh. She yelled at Ms Woods to stop.

Pearly felt a tug on the end of her rope. She pulled on the rope to alert Stanley and Ms Woods that she was stuck.

The rope flew back into her face.

Just rope.

With no Stanley attached.

CHAPTER 23

In the thick white mist, Pig didn't see Pearly stuck in the snow, so he bumped right into her, toppling over and landing – *kerplunk* – in a deep mound of fresh snow. He was buried, neck deep, with only his head poking out into the blizzard.

Pearly held up the rope to Pig's face. Pig looked at the rope. He looked at Pearly. Then they both opened their mouths and screamed.

"Ms Woods! Stannnnn-leeeeey!"

SQUEAL! SQUEAL!

But it was no use. They couldn't hear them. They couldn't see them. So they couldn't find them.

Pig thrashed about, trying desperately to escape the snowy trap. But that only made matters worse, and he sank further and further into the snow until only the tips of his pink ears poking through the hood of his polar jacket were visible.

That sent Pearly into a panic. She wrenched herself

out of the snowdrift, fell to her knees at Pig's side and started digging.

"Stay still," she ordered. "I'm digging you out."

Luckily, the snow was fresh and was easy to scoop out, her enormous gloves acting like leather shovels. In seconds, she had made a wide hole around Pig's front trotters, and Pig scrambled out, oinking and bucking his back legs in distress.

They both stood staring at each other for a while, their chests heaving, their breath shooting clouds of white fog into the already white fog.

They were alone.

In the middle of Antarctica.

In an almighty blizzard.

It was clear that Ms Woods and Stanley had kept going. Ms Woods was so self-absorbed and Stanley so wheezy and sneezy, they may not have even noticed that they were no longer tied together.

Was this a good thing or a bad thing?

Pearly felt a shiver start in her arms. Her teeth banged against each other, chattering louder than a troop of chimpanzees. Pig too was twitching with cold. They were both wet from their falls in the snow and they'd stayed still for too long. This was a dangerous mix.

"We have to keep going," chattered Pearly. "Like Ms Woods said. Can you sniff her, Pig?"

Pig put his quivering snout to the ground. A worrying circle of blue ringed each nostril.

Can't smell anything, Pig wailed. *Maybe my sniffer is dud!*

"Not dud, just frozen, I think," said Pearly. "We have to keep moving."

Pearly looked about her. All she could see through the relentless snowfall was an endless white landscape. It all looked the same. She had no idea which way Ms Woods and Stanley had gone. As much as she didn't trust Ms Woods, she knew that she needed her in order to survive.

She spun around on the spot with her eyes closed and her finger pointing out in front. When she opened her eyes, she said, *This way*, and started off in the direction her finger was pointing. It might have been the wrong way, but they couldn't stay put. "Stay close," she said, and held tight to the rope that linked her to Pig.

The snow became deeper.

The wind became stronger.

The air was so sharp and cold that each breath Pearly took felt as if she was swallowing razor blades.

But they plodded on, for what seemed like hours. The blizzard was showing no sign of letting up and there was no sign of the others either. Pearly couldn't shake the feeling that perhaps Stanley had untied the rope and abandoned them on purpose. Would Stanley do that? Was he just as beastly as Ms Woods? Pearly didn't have the energy to think too much about it. She was struggling. She had a cracking headache and her lungs felt as though something was wrapped tight around them, squeezing hard. She was getting weaker by the second. It was a massive struggle to lift each foot out of the deep snow, her pack weighing her down as if it was filled with rocks.

Finally, Pearly couldn't take another step.

She let go of the rope and flopped sideways into the snow.

CHAPTER 24

OINK! SQUEAL! SQUEAK! GRUNTITY-GRUNT. SQUEAKITY-SQUEAK. OINKITY, OINKITY, OINK! cried Pig, which was pig for *What the heck are you doing? Do you want to die or something? You heard what Ms Woods said – we have to keep moving.*

"I can't," Pearly wheezed.

You have to, oinked Pig. He kicked and snorted and AROOed. Then, snout to the ground, he trotted around in circles, trying to sniff out a solution through his frozen nostrils.

Pearly had never before felt so helpless – which was saying something! Helpless and hopeless. They should be her middle names. She curled herself into a ball, snow mounding around her.

SQUEAL! SQUEAK! SQUEAK! Pig came galloping through the snow and prodded her back with his snout. *A cave,* he oinked. *I've found a cave.*

"A cave?" Pearly squinted through the snow.

She couldn't see anything except snow and fog.

Follow me! Pig tried to lift her up off the snow with his snout.

"OK! OK!" Pearly staggered to her feet and trudged through the knee-deep snow, following Pig.

And sure enough, he led her to an icy ledge jutting out of a sheer cliff that created a tiny icy space like a cave. An icy space where they could shelter from the blizzard and get their energy back.

The two of them squeezed into the small space. Pearly wrapped her arms around Pig's back to help keep him warm, her own worries wrapping themselves around her, keeping her insides fluttering.

To Pearly's dismay, it wasn't long before it started – that awful rising panic. It had happened once before, when she was stuck in the tunnel that led from Woe Mansion to the Lemon Tree River jetty. And she had felt twinges of it when hiding in the broom cupboard on the *Mighty Muncher*.

She held her breath and told herself to stop it. She told herself that this was the best place to be – out of that blizzard, away from that frenzied wind. But slowly, panic ballooned up into Pearly's chest, growing larger and larger and making her feel as if she couldn't breathe, as if she might suffocate right here and now.

The panicky balloon pressed hard against her ribs. It felt as if a colossal condor was trapped inside her and was desperate to break out. She tried to calm her breathing. She tried to whistle "Waltzing Matilda". She tried to think about her favourite things like Maria in *The Sound of Music*. But still that panicky condor stretched its wings inside her, flapping frantically.

Beside her, Pig was perfectly still. So still Pearly worried that maybe he had turned into a porky ice cube. Which only made her panic all the more.

Be calm, Pig soothed. *We've got this.*

But there was no soothing Pearly.

She had to get out – NOW! Too bad if there was a nightmarish blizzard outside that threatened to blow her away. Too bad if she might freeze to death. Too bad if she might get buried alive. It was better than being stuck in this tiny space where she couldn't get any air.

Stay here, Pig oinked, shuffling himself around so he blocked her way.

"I can't!" Pearly hissed.

Pearly wiggled. She jiggled. She wormed her way past Pig until, finally, she got one leg out into the snow.

Pearly's panic immediately eased. But her calm was short-lived.

Because something grabbed hold of her leg and pulled it, and Pearly with it, right out of the cave!

CHAPTER 25

By the time Pearly had staggered to her feet, Pig too had leaped from the cave, squealing his annoyance.

But his squealing stopped when he noticed who, or rather *what*, was standing before them.

There, towering over the pair, was an enormous fur coat.

Yes. That's right – a fur coat.

A brown and black stripy fur coat, buttoned down the front and tied with sailor's rope.

Pearly pulled up her goggles, which were foggy and had filled up with snow from her tumble out of the cave, and squinted at the furry being in front of her.

It was hard to see through the driving snow and heavy fog, but Pearly detected a woolly beanie, with knitted horns, poking out of the neck of the coat, and a pair of black snow boots sticking out from the bottom.

Was this the creature they had been searching for? Was this the Great Hairy Beast?

Pig must have been thinking the same thing, as he immediately started sniffing at the creature's feet, despite his sniffer being frozen and not working properly.

Human, oinked Pig.

Human? This was the strangest and largest human Pearly had ever seen.

Just then, a gloved hand shot out from the sleeve of the coat and latched onto Pearly's arm. It felt more like a mechanical claw than a human hand, and it had a strong hold from which Pearly was unable to escape.

The fur coat started walking – long, striding steps – dragging Pearly with it.

Pig followed close behind, squealing his distress – a piggy SOS into the snowy emptiness. Pearly hoped that someone would hear him – Ms Woods, Stanley, anyone. She didn't like her chances of getting away from this beast – fur coat or Great Hairy Beast or whatever it was – without help. Its grip was vice-like. Pearly writhed about like an angry snake, snow rolling over her, filling her goggles again and sometimes her mouth, her pack banging painfully against her back. But the fur coat kept striding purposefully, only deviating to avoid the occasional protruding rock.

The enormous fur coat dragged Pearly into a narrow crevasse. It was barely wide enough for the creature to fit through and at times it had to swing sideways to avoid scraping its shoulders. But the crevasse was sheltered from the wind. Through the still foggy air, Pearly could make out the steep craggy sides rising skyward on either side of her. She glanced around to make sure Pig was keeping up and was relieved to find him trotting close behind, puffing out steamy clouds of breath and gazing up at the vertical rock faces that flanked them.

The crevasse was long but eventually it tapered and closed up. A dead end. Fear shot through Pearly. What did the enormous fur coat want with her?

The fur coat stopped. It let go of Pearly's arm. Pearly rubbed at her arm, trying to rid herself of the feel of that mechanical claw, as a strange hissing sound echoed around her. The sheer rocky end of the crevasse wobbled. An earthquake? A landslide? A rock fall? Pearly wasn't going to wait around to find out. She was getting out of there, and fast.

"Run!" she screamed to Pig. But before she could take a single step, that gloved claw shot out and grabbed hold of her again and hauled her towards the wobbling rock face, which now seemed to be splitting in two. Definitely an earthquake! The fur coat turned sideways and slid through a thin crack where the cliff had opened up, pulling Pearly with it. Brave Pig followed. There was another hiss and a wobble and the crack closed up.

And they were in darkness.

"Pig, are you there?" Pearly whispered into the gloom.

Yes, oinked Pig, his oink as wobbly as that rock face.

There was a sharp click followed by an electric buzz and suddenly the space was flooded with light.

Pearly blinked several times against the glare. They were in a huge cavern. A very comfortable huge cavern, actually, with a sofa and table, a kitchen with a fridge, stove and microwave, and a wall of bookshelves stuffed with hundreds of books. There were even rugs on the ground. It was like a house. The enormous fur coat stood in the middle of the space.

Pearly was confused. Part of her was sure that she was standing in the lair of the Great Hairy Beast, but another part of her suspected that the fur coat wasn't the hairy beast, but something else entirely. "Who are you?" she asked, her voice a shaky whisper.

There was no answer. That gloved claw shot out again and Pearly stepped back, her brows drawn together with alarm. But it didn't reach for Pearly. Instead, it untied the coat's rope and undid the buttons.

Pearly watched with her mouth wide open in astonishment, blobs of snow sliding off her and puddling on the ground.

The coat slid off the creature's shoulders to reveal...

Another, smaller fur coat beneath. The claw unbuttoned this coat to reveal...

Another coat.

157

And then another.

Layer upon layer of coats made of some kind of fake fur that filled the cavern with a horrible synthetic smell.

All hanging from an elaborate mechanical skeleton made from steel.

And beneath it all, standing on a platform in the middle of the skeleton, was a man. A rather short and terribly thin man, wearing only a beanie, a pair of woolly long johns and knee-high snow boots. He had a thin plaited beard swinging from his chin, and wet wisps of grey hair stuck out from under his horned beanie. An excited gleam lit his eyes.

The man climbed down the legs of the skeleton and then beamed at Pearly and Pig. "Greetings, young girl and her fine pink pig," he said, taking off his beanie, swirling it in a flourish and bowing low. "And welcome." He brushed some snow off his boots, pulled a striped housecoat from a hook on the wall and slipped it on, seemingly unembarrassed that he had welcomed them in his underwear.

Pearly gazed at the man, lost for words. The man gazed back.

Pig huddled close to Pearly's legs. She could feel him trembling. "Who ... who ... are you and what is this place?" she asked finally.

"I am..." The man stopped. He bit his lip, then sighed. "I am a secret. Well, I *was* a secret, but now

I am ... not. I am exposed. A secret no more." He sat on a kitchen stool and hung his head.

Pearly was puzzled. The man had gone from excited to welcoming to sad in a matter of minutes. Pearly had no idea what to say.

"But it is what it is." The man sighed again and slid from the stool. "Where are my manners? You two have been through quite an ordeal. You must be tired and cold and hungry. Please, take a seat." He passed Pearly two woolly rugs. "Snuggle up in these. Would you like something to eat? I make a mean pizza. Vegetarian, of course," he said and winked at Pig.

Pizza! squealed Pig.

Pearly looked around her.

She was in a hidden cave in the middle of Antarctica. No one knew where she was.

And she was pretty sure that no one knew about this man – this very strange man.

She should have felt fearful. She should have been looking for a trap. Or a catch. Or at the very least – *a way out.*

But all she could think about was how this might be her lucky break. Could this be her chance to get help for her parents? Surely this man must have a way to contact the outside world.

CHAPTER 26

The man, who told Pearly to call him Prof (short for Professor), placed the pizza trays in the middle of one of the rugs and they all sat down together to eat. Pearly passed pieces to Pig, who wolfed them down in two gulps. The pizzas were delicious, and Prof didn't raise an eyebrow at eating with a pig – it was as if it was the most normal thing in the world.

It would have been a wonderful underground cavern picnic, if not for Pearly's jitters, which had her shifting position and fussing over Pig and glancing around the cavernous home, looking for a radio or telephone or computer – anything that she could use to contact someone to get help for her parents.

"You seem a bit distracted, Miss Pearly," Prof said as he handed her a steaming mug of hot chocolate and Pig his tenth helping of pizza.

"I ... I..." She had no idea how to broach the subject. The last thing she wanted to do was upset Prof and blow yet another opportunity. She had blown too many chances already – in fact, she was proving quite talented at it. But she realized that contacting someone outside Prof's hideaway bunker would mean revealing his secret – and she was pretty sure he wouldn't want that. "I ... I get that you want no one to know about your hideout here, Prof," she said finally, "but why did you risk your secret by rescuing Pig and me?"

Prof curled his beard plait around his pointer finger. "I didn't want to," he said, which surprised Pearly. "And I wouldn't have. Except for the matter of not having a choice. I couldn't watch you die out there in that blizzard. Fiercest one I've seen for decades. And I certainly couldn't trust that Ms Woods to save you."

"You know her?"

"Of course. I know everything. Haven't you worked that out yet? I had you pegged as a clever one." He sighed with disappointment, then looked at her sideways. "I've been watching you, you know, since you landed near Adlam Glacier."

"You've been watching us all that time? How?" Pearly sat upright as she recalled those moments when she'd felt that someone was there, watching.

Prof's wrinkly face split into a wide wrinkly grin. "I have my ways. And don't think you can worm any more information out of me – I do have some secrets to protect, you know. Even if I am exposed."

He did have secrets, and that was the crux of Pearly's problem. How could she convince him to help her? She chewed her bottom lip, trying to come up with the right words.

"It doesn't seem possible," Pearly tried, baiting him.

Prof chuckled. "I know. I know. It's mind boggling, isn't it? But don't try to work it out. Acceptance is the key here. It's enough to know that I have ways to protect my little patch, and that not much slips past me." Prof slid his legs out in front of him and leaned back on outstretched arms. A mischievous gleam lit his eyes. "There was another reason I rescued you though."

Pearly's eyebrows shot up. "Was it Ms Woods? Were you rescuing us from her?"

"That is true. Maybe you are a clever one after all, Miss Pearly. Her face was familiar to me when she stepped ashore, so I did a bit of detective work, a spot of spying to find out why."

Pearly's mind whirred. Did he say *spying*? Had he been creeping around their camp? Pearly found herself edging to the side of the rug.

"I checked out my newspaper and TV news archives and turns out I'd seen her on the telly, many moons ago," Prof continued. "She has a black soul, doesn't she? What's a big game hunter doing here? And what's she doing with that high-powered rifle? That's what I want to know."

"You saw her rifle? When?" Pearly asked.

Prof didn't answer. He clamped his lips closed, his eyes twinkling with mischief.

Pearly's skin was crawling. This was getting rather unnerving.

"I don't trust her one iota," Prof said finally. "Never trust anyone who seeks to harm another creature, I say."

Never trust anyone who admits they've been spying on you, thought Pearly.

Pig's ears were twitching and Pearly could tell that he had been listening in. He left the final piece of pizza and sat between Pearly and Prof, AROOing softly.

"I think she wanted to kill the Great Hairy Beast," Pearly said carefully.

Prof threw his head back and laughed. "The Great Hairy Beast? I suppose that's me, is it?"

"I think it might be. My mother, Angel Woe, has tried to find you – or the beast – too."

"Ah! It all makes sense now. Your mother is Angel Woe? She is a mighty fine tracker, I have to say. She came darn close to finding me more than once. I had to hole up in this bunker for weeks till she left. I actually retired the suit for some years, because she was getting too close to discovering my secret." Prof twirled his beard in thought. "I only used the suit for a bit of a decoy while I was setting up here. Got people fussing

163

about some mythical beast on the west coast, so they wouldn't notice the real me coming and going here in the east. Well, fancy meeting Angel Woe's daughter – that is a surprise of grand proportions."

This man knew far too much. But Pearly was not going to let that get in her way. Because here was her chance. "I think my mum, Angel, is in danger," she said. "And my dad. I think Ms Woods kidnapped them and locked them up in a warehouse in Port Clementine." Pearly choked back a sob. Her fingers trembled. "I've been trying to get help for over a week – they asked me to help them and I haven't been able to. You are my last chance. Can you? Can you please?"

Prof made a clicking sound with his tongue. He twisted his lips to one side. "Can I *what*?"

"Can you call or radio the police in Orchard Island or the people at the station at Finn Bay and let them know? I worry for their–"

"Hang on. Hang on. Hang on. Slow down. No, actually. I can't."

"I know it might threaten your secret, but surely we can think of a way..."

"No, Miss Pearly. That's not it. I can't because I can't. I don't have a radio or anything. That's the point of a secret hideaway – to hide away from the outside world. And that means having absolutely no communication. I'm sorry."

Pearly pushed herself to her feet.

Mamma mia!

Why couldn't things work out for her, for once?

She'd had enough. Her cheeks were on fire and so was her temper. "That's not true!" she yelled, her jaw clenched, her hands fists by her sides. "You must have some way to contact people! You're lying, just to protect your secret."

She began pacing and muttering in Italian. Prof put his arm around her shoulder. She shrugged it off and continued pacing.

"Hey, hey, calm yourself down," Prof said patiently and guided her to the sofa. "Please sit." He handed her a handkerchief as she plonked down on the sofa. "Look, my secret is important to me. But not so important that I would jeopardize the life of another living being. I saved you, didn't I? And I am telling the truth. Really. We'll simply have to think of another plan."

Pearly blew her nose and wiped her eyes. She didn't know whether to trust this strange little man. But regardless of whether he was telling the truth or not, Pearly couldn't get past the thought that she had failed, yet again. This bunker was not their lucky break at all. For all she knew, Prof might hold them prisoner.

They might be stuck here in his icy underground bunker for ever.

His slave.

His experiment.

His...

An ear-splitting squeal filled the bunker.

Pig was on his feet and turning in circles, his snout held high.

Bear! he oinked. *My sniffer is thawed and I can smell pizza and human and POLAR BEAR!*

CHAPTER 27

"What's wrong with your pig?" Prof leaped up, his brows scrunched together.

"His snout is working again," sniffled Pearly, swiping the wetness from her chin.

"His snout?" said Prof.

"Yes. *We* have secrets too." There was a brittle edge to her voice. "He can detect and identify the scent of every animal known to man."

"Intriguing. Is that why he's here? To sniff out this Great Hairy Beast?"

"Yes. And right now he is telling me he can smell – bear. Polar bear!"

"Oh dang," said Prof. "I was hoping to keep that little secret a secret." Prof's face drooped with sadness. "I must be losing my touch." Then he snapped his head up and fixed Pearly with an astonished gaze. "You understood the pig! How is that possible?"

"It's just something that I've always been able to

do. I have a talent for languages." Pearly was tired of secrets. Besides, what use was keeping her family's deep dark secret when she might not ever see her family again? She swallowed hard and blinked back tears.

"I thought there was something odd about the two of you – the way you interacted. Golly Molly, this is getting more and more curious." Prof tugged on his plait.

"You're telling me," said Pearly. "You have a polar bear here, in Antarctica?" Pearly couldn't believe what she was hearing. Those prints *were* actually bear prints. "How did you get a polar bear here? That's horrible."

"Oh no, no, no. No conclusion jumping, please. I would never take an animal from its natural environment. That's one of the reasons I'm holed up here. So I can watch and learn and enjoy all the wildlife without getting in the way. I didn't bring the bear here. It came all by itself."

"That's impossible," said Pearly. She was finding it increasingly difficult to believe anything this man said. He was far too full of secrets.

"Apparently not," said Prof. "Because I have one – right here."

Pig was sniffing around the room and taking a good long whiff near the wall lined with bookshelves. *Strongest here*, he oinked.

"When you say you have one here – do you mean you have one, like, *right* here?"

"Sadly, yes. It goes against all that I believe in, but yes, I have a polar bear here in my bunker."

Prof plodded to the wall where Pig was sniffing and snorting with gusto. He put his hand against the spine of a book and the shelves slid open. "Yep, the old secret passage behind the bookshelf trick." A twinkle lit his eye. "Why invent something new when films have already got it covered? Follow me."

He led them down a wide passage fashioned out of bare rock. It was barely tall enough for Prof to walk without stooping, and was strangely warm, dimly lit and smelt like wet socks. It reminded Pearly of the tunnels through the cliff from Woe Mansion to the river, and she had to fight the feeling that the walls were closing in and trying to squeeze against her. She wrapped her arms across her middle to stop them from shaking.

"How did you make all this?" she asked, bewildered, taking in the closed metal doors dotted along the rough rock walls.

"I have my ways," Prof replied. Pearly rolled her eyes and sighed. "And time. I've had plenty of time. Years and years of time."

"You have all of *this*," Pearly waved her arms around the passageway, "but no way to contact the outside world?" She didn't try to hide her disappointment.

"I have upset you, I know. But believe me, if I had a way to help you help your parents, I would."

At the end of the passage, Prof produced a key from the pocket of his housecoat and unlocked a large arched door. He beckoned them inside.

Pearly hesitated. She wasn't sure about this secretive man any more. But Pig pushed past her and trotted inside.

The room stank of fish guts. A few steps in front of them was a wall made of metal bars, like that of a jail cell or enormous cage. Behind the bars, the rocky ground gave way to a large pit, with a few boulders, a murky pool and – a polar bear.

The skinniest, most miserable-looking polar bear Pearly had ever seen. It was perched on top of the largest boulder, its head on its front paws, its ribcage clearly visible beneath its mangy creamy-white coat.

Pig squealed in distress.

Pearly rushed to the bars. "This is cruel!" she hissed. "How could you?"

"It is terrible; it is the truth," said Prof. "And what is an even more terrible truth is that she is starving herself. I've watched her for weeks and she hasn't gone anywhere near the shore. She hasn't eaten a single thing. She's wasting away to nothing."

"Poor thing." Pearly took in her surroundings – the miserable-looking polar bear, locked in a room that was no more than a large prison – a large animal prison. This was unsettling at best.

"When your Ms Woods came along, intent on finding me – the beast, the bear, whatever – I had to act quickly." Pearly shuddered to think what Ms Woods would have done if she had spotted a polar bear. A polar bear in Antarctica. That would certainly be a prize kill for someone like her. That would get her on the front page of *BIG GAME* magazine and also on the *News at Six*, no doubt.

Pearly frowned. "And you just happen to have an animal prison in your secret bunker."

"Not a prison. A place for injured animals to heal," he replied evenly. "It was one of the first things I made – though it's been rather useless. I've only had the need to use it twice before."

The polar bear let out a low mournful groan that made Pearly's eyes well. "How did you get her in here?" she asked, still suspicious. "Don't polar bears like to eat people?"

"I have my ways," said Prof.

"Sheesh. Enough with the secrets – I've told you plenty of mine!"

"OK," he said. "Think tranquillizer gun and fork-lift skidoo." Pig *AROO*ed at the mention of the tranquillizer gun and Pearly rubbed his back in sympathy. "I only got her in a few hours ago – in the wee hours of the morning. I couldn't chance her being out in the open once I worked out who Ms Woods was." Prof studied the bear with worry in his eyes. "It was an easier job than expected – she's very frail. I don't think she could have attacked me even if she wanted to."

Pearly knew this too was the truth. The bear hadn't even raised her head to acknowledge their presence. She was floppy and weak – scarily so.

"I've been trying to feed her some fish, but she's not interested. It's as if she's given up hope. I don't know what to do."

"I can talk to her if you like," said Pearly, regretting the words as they came tumbling out of her mouth.

"You speak polar bear?"

"Not really. Well, a little. I listened to some in a documentary a few months ago about climate change and the ice caps melting. They sounded pretty similar to elk, but with a bit of brown bear mixed in – I should be able to understand some things. If she wants to talk, that is."

"Brilliant!" said Prof. "This was meant to be. I knew something good would come out of the Great Pearly and Pig Rescue. Fire away!"

CHAPTER 28

The polar bear was reluctant to talk at first. And in truth, Pearly was reluctant too. She couldn't stop thinking about whether Prof was telling the truth about having no communication in his bunker. Who would do that? What about emergencies? The bunker had power and appliances, heating and light – it had a secret passageway behind a bookshelf, for goodness sake, and an entrance in a crevasse. But no way to communicate with the outside world? It didn't make sense. Why did Prof want to cut himself off like that? What did he have to hide?

Pearly perched on a stool in front of the metal bars. She hated animals in cages, loathed zoos, and this didn't make it any easier for her to connect with the poor miserable bear. She pulled her legs up onto the stool and rested her chin on top of her knees. She relaxed her face and smiled, and then started with a few basic chuffs and gravelly growls.

The bear ignored her – she didn't even raise her head. She let out a short breathy huff that stank of hunger and rotten fish, and which Pearly took as a scoff. Pearly was winging it, drawing on instinct and bits of brown bear and elk she'd heard on a hike in Montana when she was nine.

The more she tried, the more she worried for the bear, and the more she worried for the bear, the less she obsessed about Prof and the bunker and how she was failing her parents. And eventually, she won the bear over.

The bear rolled onto her side, stood on wobbly legs and shook herself fiercely. She opened her mouth wide, showing off her impressive fangs and filling the room with an exasperated roar, which made Prof step towards the door and Pig duck under the stool. But Pearly didn't flinch. She kept an even gaze and chuffed softly.

The bear roared once more, then plodded clumsily off the boulder and came to sit opposite Pearly. She was ready to talk.

Understanding the bear was more difficult than Pearly had imagined. Her name was Char – or something like that. Pearly couldn't be sure. By the time Pearly had worked that out, she was red faced and hot, and regretting her boast that she could communicate with a polar bear. It took nearly another hour for Pearly to piece together Char's story.

When she was finished, Char clambered back up onto her boulder and lay down, her head on her paws. She was asleep in seconds.

Prof held open the door and Pearly and Pig followed him along the dank passage and out through the secret doorway into the living area. Pearly flopped onto the sofa with Pig, relieved to be out of the tunnel. Prof settled himself into an armchair. Then Pearly told them Char's story, even though she wasn't sure she had it right.

As far as Pearly could work out, Char had been asleep on pack ice that broke away and floated out of her bay. Char didn't realize what had happened until her patch of ice was in the middle of the ocean with no land in sight. Pearly wasn't exactly certain what happened next, except that eventually the ice melted, and somehow Char ended up hiding on a lifeboat that hung from the side of a ship. She thought the ship would take her back home. When she finally sighted an icy glacier spilling into the sea, she launched herself into the bay and swam ashore. But once she got to shore she was attacked by hundreds of the noisiest, strangest feathered animals she had ever seen. They came for her. Straight at her. She panicked.

"She's afraid of the penguins," Pearly told Prof and Pig. "That's why she won't go near the sea. It's the penguins – they terrify her. She thought she was in Alaska, so she is very confused about the scary birds."

Pearly curled into the sofa. She was exhausted. Communicating with Char had been exhausting. Add to that getting lost in a blizzard and being dragged through the snow by an enormous fur coat, and she was done in. Her eyelids drooped. Her head thumped. She wanted to sleep for a thousand hours.

But Prof had other ideas. "Penguins!" He pressed his fingertips together and tapped his chin. "Penguins! I am a secret no more, but I am more wise than before. And wisdom is valuable. Penguins en masse are noisy, and I suspect very intimidating for a polar bear who has never seen one before, let alone hundreds. Poor Char. No wonder—" Prof stopped mid-sentence. He leaned forwards in his chair and bent his head to one side, as if listening. "I say, do you hear that?" He leaped to his feet.

"No. I don't hear anything," Pearly said wearily.

"That, Miss Pearly, is exactly the point. The sharp end of the stick."

Prof wasn't making any sense, but then, Pearly had come to realize, he often didn't. He rushed to the wall beside the heater, where a long straight pipe climbed up the rocky wall and disappeared into the ceiling. He pulled a lever and another much shorter pipe shot out at a right angle. Prof threaded his hair behind his ears and put one eye to the pipe. "Aha! Will you look at that?" Prof danced on the spot.

"What?"

"Come see. Quick now."

Pearly dragged herself from the sofa and tramped across to the strange contraption that was making Prof all fizzy. She placed one eye against the short horizontal pipe, as Prof had done, and was amazed when a snowy and very familiar landscape appeared. This wasn't a pipe; it was some kind of peephole – like a periscope on a submarine.

"See!" said Prof. "The blizzard has passed and now it is time for us to get cracking!"

Pearly was bewildered. "Get cracking?"

"Yes. Of course. We need to get Char back to the Arctic, and you need to call for help for your parents. What are you waiting for?"

CHAPTER 29

Prof was infuriating. Tight-lipped. Cagey. Annoying. If Pearly heard him say, "I have my ways" or "you'll see" one more time, she was going to scream. Sure, he wanted to keep his secret a secret. Sure, he was feeling exposed. But how was she meant to carry out this plan when she had no idea what the plan was? Her own plans might lack detail at times, but Prof's plan had no detail – or at least, no detail that he cared to share with her and Pig.

They were in the smelly secret passageway behind the bookshelf again. Prof had lumbered off ahead, his housecoat flapping, disappearing through another hidden door. He reappeared several minutes later riding a skidoo. Behind it was a long trailer packed high with goodness knows what. The machine almost scraped both walls of the tunnel and Prof had to negotiate a twenty-point turn to get it into the passageway and pointing towards Char's prison room.

"Hop on!" Prof called cheerfully.

They obeyed, and Pearly and Pig huddled together on a narrow bench seat at the back of the trailer.

"Hold tight!"

Prof revved the skidoo, and the tunnel filled with the smell of petrol. Pig snorted and Pearly coughed. Prof cheered, then sent the skidoo zooming along the dimly lit passageway.

He could be taking us to a dark damp dungeon, Pearly fretted. *Or perhaps to a stasis chamber in a secret lab. Or maybe he is going to deliver us back into the hands of Ms Woods and Stanley Snell...* That condor seemed intent on opening its wings inside her chest again.

Pig sensed her unease. *I don't smell trouble, Pearly. If that helps,* Pig oinked, above the roar of the skidoo, which echoed all around them in the tight space.

Her mother's words came back to her: *Pig's snout never lies.* Angel had been right so far. Pig's snout had been spot on, even when it was almost frozen solid. Pearly tried to thrust her worries into a box in her brain and shut the lid tight. She had to. There was too much at stake.

The skidoo screeched to a halt. Prof jumped off and opened a door in the wall with his key. Char's prison.

"What's keeping you, Miss Pearly? Come now. Time is ticking. Tell Char to come with you. I've made space in the trailer for her."

Pearly jumped down from her seat. Pig followed.

"We're taking Char with us?" she asked.

Prof's eyebrows shot up his forehead. "Ye-es – how else are we going to get her home?" he said, as if rescuing polar bears and taking them from one ice cap to the other was an everyday occurrence.

"Do you think that's safe?" Pearly asked.

"Let's hope so," said Prof.

That wasn't exactly reassuring. Pearly plodded inside, and Prof unlocked the metal gate. Pearly held on to the bars, pressed her face through them as far as it could go, and chuffed and huffed and coughed and tried to cajole a sceptical Char out of her jail.

Char moved slowly and awkwardly to the top of the highest boulder. Pearly chewed her bottom lip with worry. Char was so weak, every step seemed to take much effort. They had to get her home – and fast. Char sat back on her haunches, raised her front paws up, tilted her head back and let out a lion-like roar.

"She won't go," said Pearly. "It's the penguins."

Prof propped the cage door open. "Tell her there will be no penguins," he said.

"How can you be sure?" Pearly asked.

"I can't. But she doesn't need to know that."

Mamma mia! Pearly didn't like the sound of that, and she didn't like fibbing to a polar bear – especially one she was going to be sharing the back of a trailer with. She looked to Pig, who twitched his ears and oinked, *No choice.*

So Pearly tried to find the noises that told Char there would be no penguins and that Prof was going to take her home, and eventually Char clambered down the boulders, through the murky pond and out of the gate.

Prof rearranged a few items on the trailer, then Char climbed on board and sat erect behind Pearly and Pig.

Pearly could feel her hot breath on her neck, and even though she was fond of Char and felt sorry for her, sitting this close to an animal that high up on the food chain made her jittery.

"And we're off!" yelled Prof.

Char growled.

Pig *AROO*ed.

Pearly held on tight, muttering to herself in Italian.

Prof navigated the unusual band of travellers through a series of interconnecting tunnels. The tunnels swung to the right, then to the left. Pearly knew that she would get hopelessly lost if she had to find her own way back. She also knew that kilometres of ice lay on top of the rock in some places in Antarctica, and that fact hung as heavily as the rocky ceiling above her.

Every now and again, Prof stopped, jumped off and pulled a lever on the wall. One of his periscope contraptions would appear, Prof would take a look and exclaim "All good!" or "Perfect!" or "Nearly there!" before taking off again.

So this was how Prof had watched them, Pearly decided. These periscopes gave him eyes everywhere. It was a creepy thought.

At last they stopped and Prof called out, "Everyone off. This is it."

Pearly was glad to get off – she was getting a cramp in her legs, her feet had pins and needles, and Char's stinky fish guts breath was getting hard to handle. Besides, she was dying to know what "it" was.

"Get your stuff. And get Char ready."

Mamma mia! "Ready for what?" Pearly asked.

Prof ignored her. He pulled a wall lever and peered through another one of his periscopes. "Dang!" he muttered. "Dang, dang, dang. Double, double, double dang. Dang."

Pearly's arms prickled. "What's the matter?" she asked.

Prof peered through the periscope again. He twirled his thin plaited beard. He scratched his scalp. He stamped his booted foot.

Then he looked from Pearly to Pig to Char, screwed his mouth to one side and said, "There is only one way. I didn't want it. But there is no other."

Pearly wished he would stop talking in riddles and tell them what was going on.

Prof threw the plastic cover off the back of the trailer to reveal the mechanical skeleton and a bag of smelly fake fur coats.

"What's going on?" Pearly demanded.

"Take a look for yourself." Prof indicated the periscope, as he tugged the skeleton off the trailer sideways to avoid Char.

Pearly put her eye to the cylinder pipe. The blizzard had certainly abated. The wind had sculpted the polar landscape and it was eerily still after the ferocious gale that they had tramped through. But all she could see was snow, snow and more snow, a glistening white carpet of snow.

"So, there's snow..." Pearly said.

Prof sighed.

He propped the frame against the seat at the back of the trailer and reached across to adjust the cylinder on the periscope. "Take another look," he said.

OINKY OINKY NO-NO, oinked Pig as Pearly put her eye to the scope again.

The view had changed slightly.

There was a rocky outcrop with spear-like icicles hanging from the exposed rock. There were deep windswept snowdrifts, and jagged triangles of ice sticking up from the edge of a glacier, like enormous shark's teeth, and there were...

Two people plodding through the thick snow.

One striding ahead with a rifle slung over her shoulder.

One hunched over and wobbly, holding a camera with both hands.

The big game hunter and her photographer!

CHAPTER 30

"Time is not to be lost," Prof muttered, as he dragged the metal skeleton up a sloping path in the tunnel towards a closed hatch cut in the rock wall. "No other way."

"What are you doing?" Pearly demanded. She took another look at Ms Woods and Stanley, who were bent over and ploughing through the deep snow. They both looked exhausted.

OINKY OINKY NO-NO, oinked Pig, pacing beside the periscope. OINKY OINKY NO-NO.

Prof twisted a dial on the hatch and opened it out. A blast of cold air whooshed into the tunnel. Light flooded in. "There is no other way. No other way."

He reached for the skeleton, but Pearly grabbed it first.

"Stop," she said, exasperated. "What *is* the plan? We don't know what you're doing."

"A decoy. I was a secret and now I am the decoy. There is no other way." His face was stricken, turned wet

185

and grey with worry. His plaited beard dripped sweat. "A secret no more. Exposed. And now a decoy." He was working himself into a state. "*You* have to do it now."

"Please, Prof, make some sense. What do I have to do?"

"The plan. Get help for your parents and save Char."

"But how? How do I do that?"

Prof shoved the skeleton out through the hatch onto the snow outside. "Finn Bay Station. They will radio for help. They will look after Char. They are good people. They will do the right thing."

"But where is it? I can't find the station alone." Italian phrases hissed and spat inside Pearly's head.

"You must." He beckoned Pearly to the scope. He adjusted it slightly and then held it out to her. "There. Take a look – see the gorilla?"

A gorilla? The Prof was definitely going mad! But then, if there was a polar bear, why not a gorilla? Pearly squinted into the scope, searching for a gorilla in the snow. "No gorillas," she said, her voice soft.

"Look properly," said Prof. "That rocky outcrop rising out of the ice to the east. See it? Look at it with an open mind. That's Gorilla Rock."

Pearly zeroed in on the strange arrangement of rocky boulders and jagged peaks. She squinted. She opened her mind and there it was! One large boulder sat on top of another, making the shape of a head, with protruding eyebrows and chin. It was unmistakeably the profile of a gorilla's face. "Ah, yes, I see." But that's not all she saw. "Ms Woods and Stanley are heading straight for it."

"Correct. That is the problem. That is the why of the situation."

"But why is it the why?" Pearly rolled her eyes – she was starting to sound like Prof.

"At last – an excellent question. Whys are the most important questions of all to ask. Remember that." He collected a bundle of fur coats and began tossing them out of the hatch.

"But why?" Pearly could not contain her exasperation. "You haven't told me why yet."

Prof threw off his housecoat and swivelled around to face Pearly in his long johns. He frowned at her. "Why? *Why?* I would think that is obvious. The gorilla is in the way. Of course. Slap bang in the middle. You must go past Gorilla Rock to get to the glacier. Follow the glacier and it will take you right past the station. It's the only way."

Pearly gulped.

Pig's pacing picked up speed, his little legs going at double time. OINKY OINKY NO-NO, he oinked. OINKY OINKY NO-NO.

"You can't go out there dressed as the Great Hairy Beast," Pearly said slowly. It was starting to dawn on her what Prof was planning to do. "You can't. She has a rifle. She is a hunter. She is hunting ... you!"

"I know that. That's the plan. I am the decoy. I will show myself and lure them away. I can't let her find Char. It's the only way."

Char let out a sad howl that made Pearly wince.

This was another impossible situation. Another impossible, hopeless situation. There was nothing in the *RAG* about anything like this.

Prof tugged his horned beanie over his ears and stepped through the hatch. "Don't worry. I have played this game many times."

"It's not a game! *How* will you get away? Ms Woods will chase you down. She is a *famous* hunter. She is good at it. Skilled. She's killed rhinos and grizzlies and..."

Prof pulled at his beard and smiled. "I have my ways, Miss Pearly. I have my ways."

Pearly held her gloved hands over her mouth. She certainly hoped that he did have a way, because she knew that Ms Woods wouldn't give up once she had him in her sights.

Prof pointed to the scope. "Keep watch. As soon as those two give chase, get Pig and Char out of here and head for the gorilla. Once you get past it, you will see the way to go. It's not far."

Pearly chewed her bottom lip. "But Char – what will I tell them about Char?"

"You are a smart girl, you will work it out. Oh, but what you won't tell them is anything about me or my bunker or these tunnels. Promise?"

"Promise," Pearly said, her stomach churning, her head spinning.

"You are a smart girl and a girl with secrets of her own. A girl with secrets is a girl I can trust." Prof dipped low and gave a flourishing wave. "Farewell, Miss Pearly and Mr Pig – it has been most pleasurable to meet you."

And with that, he stepped into the Antarctic air in nothing but his long johns, beanie and boots. He shut the hatch and left Pearly alone in the tunnel with a panicky, pacing Pig and a hungry, homesick polar bear.

CHAPTER 31

Pearly fixed her eye to the periscope.

Pig paced.

Char chuffed softly.

And Ms Woods and Stanley tramped closer and closer to the cluster of rocks and boulders that formed Gorilla Rock.

Were they heading for the station or were they just lost after the blizzard? Pearly wondered. She adjusted the scope to scan its entire field of vision. Perhaps they had tramped back to the skidoo and driven it here. That was a possibility.

But there was no sign of the skidoo.

There *was* an enormous fur coat though. An enormous fur coat plodding with an awkward sway towards Gorilla Rock and Ms Woods and Stanley Snell.

Pearly's heart took up residence in her throat. Prof was literally exposed now. Right out in the open. He was risking so much...

What's happening? What's happening? oinked Pig.

"He's right behind them," Pearly said.

OINKY OINKY NO-NO! Pig whimpered.

"So do I," Pearly said under her breath. "So do I."

Pearly watched as Ms Woods stopped under the great slab of rock that hung out over the mound. She dropped her rucksack and leaned back against a large boulder, directly under the gorilla's chin, smoothing out her wavy ponytail and flicking snow from her snowsuit. She pointed at Stanley, who responded by dropping his pack, holding up his camera and moving around her – taking photos, Pearly guessed. Business as usual, it seemed. Had they even bothered to look for her and Pig at all?

Ms Woods posed for him. She shielded her eyes with one hand and tilted her chin to the sky, her rifle resting across her thighs. She dropped onto one knee and took pretend aim. She draped the rifle behind her back and pretended to scale a boulder.

It was better than watching morning cartoons. If Prof wasn't on such a dangerous mission, Pearly would have laughed out loud.

But he was – and he was getting perilously close. *What if she shoots him?* Pearly worried. *What if she captures him and finds out the beast is just a man with a plaited beard wearing long johns? What if she finds his bunker? And Char? What if—*

Ms Woods took up a new pose. This time she was pointing at something in the distance. And that's when she spotted Prof.

In an instant, she switched from model to hunter.

She crouched low, legs apart, her rifle held in front of her, ready. She said something to Stanley. Stanley switched cameras and stooped behind her, as Ms Woods started to stalk her prey.

She seemed to glide across the snow, her eyes trained on the enormous fur-coated horned creature before her. Each step was deliberate, precise.

Prof backed away, far too slowly for Pearly's liking.

Ms Woods took aim.

Pearly held her breath.

Prof wheeled around and bolted away.

Ms Woods fired. Prof swayed. Pearly watched as his enormous fur coat tilted from one side to the other, as if it might topple right over. Had he been shot?

She had to help him. She couldn't stand here and watch him be hunted. But what could she do?

Could she be a decoy too? She looked about her to see if there was anything she could throw out of the hatch to distract Ms Woods. But there was nothing. And if she threw something from here, it would only draw Ms Woods this way – which was totally counter-productive. Oh, what could she do?

She looked back through the scope. Prof was

taking long strides away from Gorilla Rock now and was heading towards a vast and very open ice field.

Ms Woods was giving chase, firing as she ran, with Stanley waddling behind.

Hurry! Hurry! urged Pearly. *Why is he heading that way? There's no cover. He'll be a sitting duck – or, in actual fact, a standing enormous fur coat.* Which meant he was an enormous target.

Prof took a zigzagging route, the coat swinging from side to side, avoiding Ms Woods's shots. Shards of ice exploded into the air around him.

Ms Woods and Stanley were starting to close in when Prof disappeared. Just like that. There one minute, gone the next. Pearly rubbed her eyes and took another look. But it was true. He wasn't anywhere to be seen.

Ms Woods and Stanley stopped in their tracks. Stanley mopped his face and blew his nose. Ms Woods prowled about, obviously bewildered too, until she pointed at something in the distance and the two clomped off out of periscope range.

Pearly gulped. She hoped that Prof was hiding. She prayed that he was safe.

But more than anything, she had to trust that *he had his ways* and he would be fine.

Because this was *their* "it".

She turned the dial on the hatch. "Come on," she said. "It's now or never."

Pig grunted with glee and trotted out into the snow.

Char didn't budge. She chuffed and huffed and coughed about the penguins. Pearly reassured her there were none, the lie sizzling on the end of her tongue, until finally, Char stepped cautiously off the trailer and out into the snow.

Pearly closed the hatch behind her.

It was all up to her now. She had to get help for her parents and save Char.

She hoped she was up to the challenge.

Because this time, failure was not an option.

CHAPTER 32

Pearly hauled her adventure pack onto her back and scanned the immense snowy land before her. There was no sign of Ms Woods or Stanley Snell. It appeared that Prof had successfully led them on a wild fur coat chase. She forced herself to believe that Prof was OK and that he would keep them away for as long as they needed. She forbade herself from even thinking about any other possibility. She had no time for worries.

The blizzard had left behind a deep layer of fresh snow. Pig pushed through it like a snowplough, sometimes almost disappearing beneath the thick white slush. But for Pearly and Char the going was much more difficult: for Pearly because sometimes her legs would sink deep into the snow; and for Char because each step seemed to zap her energy. She appeared to be getting frailer by the minute.

Pearly fixed her eyes on the unusual cluster of rocks that formed the gorilla face. This was her first marker. She didn't dare lose sight of them. If she could get them all safely past Gorilla Rock, they should be able to follow the glacier to Finn Bay Station. And to help. Could it really be true? Could she really be this close to getting help at last?

As the gorilla grew tantalizingly close, Pearly's body started tingling and Pig started oinking a warning.

Two pale brown lumps lay on the snow under the gorilla's chin. Rucksacks! Ms Woods and Stanley had rushed off in such a hurry that they had left them behind. Which meant they would be back.

"Smoky bacon!" Pearly muttered in English and then Italian.

They couldn't linger here, that's for sure.

"Come on," she urged again, just as Char plopped down onto the snow and lay her head on her paws.

Char coughed her disgust. Pearly knew Char needed to rest; she was walking with a strange limp now. But they couldn't stop here. It was too risky.

Pearly knelt beside Char and coughed and chuffed in her ear, pleading with her to get up.

Eventually, Char huffed again and staggered to her feet, then joined Pearly and Pig as they traversed over the gorilla's cheek and eye and then down the other side. They squeezed through a tight corridor between icy cliffs, until at last the glacier emerged before them.

They traipsed down a steep slope to the edges of the glacier, stumbling on pebbles and sliding on sections of ice, until at last they drew alongside the frozen river on its slow journey to the sea.

"Nearly there!" Pearly encouraged. She glanced behind them and was relieved to see that no one was following. The glacier was wide and mighty. Great frozen lumps of ice swept around a magnificent mountain peak that stretched up into the unbroken blue skies. Such a brilliant afternoon. Or was it evening? Or even night? Pearly had no idea. She couldn't wait to turn that bend, because she was pretty sure that once they did, the red buildings of Finn Bay Station would come into view. Excitement fizzed inside her.

But not for long.

Pig put his snout in the air and waved it around. He squealed softly, then trotted up beside Pearly and whisper-oinked, *Penguins. A stack of them.*

"Where?" Pearly whispered back, her eyes flitting, her chest tight.

Close by. Probably around that bend.

Pearly didn't know what to do.

She glanced about. Was there another way? On one side of the glacier, the enormous mountain rose out of the ice. On the other, a never-ending ice field stretched as far as the eye could see. The mountain was impossible to scale, especially with the condition

Char was in, and the ice field could easily see them hopelessly lost, even if they were able to navigate over the patches of jagged ice.

They had to keep close to the glacier – it was the pathway to Finn Bay Station. She willed Pig's snout to be wrong. She willed the penguins to disappear. She willed Char not to notice. But just as she had these thoughts, the air filled with the cheeps and chirps of many birds, and waddling around the bend came a procession of penguins – squawking and chattering and heading their way.

Char froze. She glared at Pearly, her black eyes accusing, and let fly with an enormous roar – so loud, Pearly feared Ms Woods would hear. And that was the last thing they needed. Prof might be able to outwit and outrun Ms Woods and her rifle, but the weakened Char had no chance.

"Shh!" warned Pearly, then launched into a series of chuffs and growls to try to calm a frightened Char.

But Char would not be calmed. She turned and loped away, terror in her eyes.

"No Char!" Pearly called. "Come back! They won't hurt you."

Pig squealed and gave chase, trying to channel his inner sheepdog and round Char up. He galloped and grunted and squealed.

Char dodged and pivoted and growled.

The pair slid around in circles.

Until finally Char tripped and went sprawling onto the ice. She slid on her belly, legs outstretched, until she came to a thumping stop in a mound of snow.

Pearly ran to her. She frantically swiped away the snow covering Char's face and neck. Char didn't move. Her breathing was fast and shallow, her body limp. *I'm sorry, Char*, Pearly tried to tell her. *I didn't want to lie.*

Char gave out a weak huff in reply, as the line of penguins toddled past them, up over some rocks and into the ice field.

Pearly tried to convince Char that the penguins were gone. But Char didn't respond. Why would she believe Pearly anyhow?

Besides, Pearly knew that Char had used up the last of her energy trying to escape the penguins. She was too weak even to stand, let alone to walk a step further.

CHAPTER 33

Pearly threw her pack off and flopped back onto the snow. She had failed. Again.

She had failed when failure was not an option. When failure meant that Char might die, that Pearly's parents might never be freed and that she and Pig might perish in the ice fields of Antarctica. That's if Ms Woods didn't find them first. The nightmarish possibilities that could mean made her whole body tremble. Prof had risked his life to save them, and all for nothing.

She wanted to scream!

She was a useless Adventurologist.

She was a hopeless daughter. *We need you, Pearly. GET HELP.*

Yeah, right. She could *not* be relied on.

Pig prodded her with his snout. *Get up,* he oinked. *Char's in a bad way.*

Pearly turned onto her side, the snow cold and wet against her cheek. "You think I don't know that?"

She needs help.

"Not exactly my strength," scowled Pearly.

Oh, stop it.

"Stop it? Stop what? If Char needs help then you better go find someone who can deliver, because I obviously can't. Ask my parents, if you don't believe me!"

The station – it's just around the bend. Pig prodded her again. *Char needs you.*

Pearly sat up and hugged her legs to her chest. "It's no use, you know that. I can't do this. I just bring disaster."

Pig started AROOing. He was getting agitated. At her. But what did he want her to do?

AROO. AROO. AROO. Pig paced beside Char. AROO. AROO. AROO.

"Will you stop that? I *have* tried. Nothing I try works!" Pearly wailed to the blue sky above.

Smoky bacon to those thoughts, Pig oinked. *Try harder.*

Pearly jumped to her feet and kicked at the snow. "*Mamma mia!* Try harder? You want me to try harder?" she yelled in Italian as she picked up fistfuls of snow and hurled them at the mighty glacier. "I'm done! I can't do this any more!"

Char chuffed and moaned.

Pearly fell to her knees, tears and snot spilling into the snow.

Pig sat beside her.

I will stay with Char, Pig oinked eventually, as if it had been decided, as if Pearly had no say in the matter. *You go to the station. You have to, Pearly. I can't. You don't want Ms Woods to find Char first.*

Pearly sighed. She was so very tired. Every bone in her body ached, even the bones in her little toes. But Pig was right. She didn't have a choice. She had to try.

"Will you be all right?" she worried.

I have to be. Hurry!

Pearly huffed gently in Char's ear, telling her to hang tight, she'd be back with help. She wasn't sure if she believed it herself. But if she didn't try, Char didn't have a chance.

She stumbled to her feet, brushed the snow from her snowsuit, gave Pig a weak grin and headed off.

CHAPTER 34

It was just as well that Char wasn't with her, Pearly thought, as she rounded the bend and trekked over a small rise. Because there, stretched out as far as she could see, was a noisy, and very smelly, ocean of penguins. Hundreds of them. Maybe thousands! Squawking. Waddling. Some sliding on their bellies. Some shaking their feathers. A mass of beaks and feathers. And great grey clusters of downy chicks, all huddled together.

Char's worst nightmare.

In truth, Pearly wasn't too thrilled either.

But beyond the penguin colony was a sight that filled Pearly with nervous hope. The low red buildings of Finn Bay Station shone at her like a beacon, only a few hundred metres away.

But first she had to get past the penguins.

Pearly tightened her grip on her adventure pack and took a few tentative steps towards the squawking mass of black and white birds. She tried to listen to the squawks to see if she could understand anything, but there was so much noise, and so many different squawks and cheeps and chirps that she couldn't make sense of any of it.

Her heart hammered in her chest. Horrible thoughts pounded her brain.

She calmed her breathing to slow her heartbeat. She gave thoughts about being attacked by those angry beaks, of being surrounded and knocked over and trampled on, a jolly good shove out of her head. *Smoky bacon to those worries!*

She could do this.

She had to do this.

Char and Pig and her parents and Prof were all depending on her.

The weight of responsibility made Pearly falter as she made her way to the edge of the colony, but as she stumbled up to the first huddle, the noisy penguins simply ignored her. In fact, they didn't just ignore her, they actually parted to let her through, and then they went about their business as if she didn't exist. She continued on, the penguins moving out of her way and giving her clear passage.

She felt like the Queen of the Penguins. It was such an exhilarating experience, she started giggling. Here she was, Pearly the failed Adventurologist, the supreme worrier, marching through an enormous penguin colony in the middle of a glacier in the middle of Antarctica, all by herself. With every step, she started to feel more and more confident.

She could do it. She *was* doing it.

Soon she had made it through, and she lumbered towards Finn Bay, the squawks and chirps of the birds becoming fainter and fainter the closer she got to the station.

The station. She couldn't believe that she had finally made it. After all that had happened, here she was, at Finn Bay Station. Finally, she should be able to alert the police about her parents and Ms Woods. And somehow, she was going to have to convince someone that there was a poorly polar bear and a pig on the other side of the mountain needing rescuing too. She had no idea how she was going to do that.

After the noise and chaos of the penguin colony, the station was deadly quiet. So much so that Pearly started to worry that maybe it was deserted.

Her mouth was dry. Her fingers trembled in her gloves. But as she put her boot on the first step of the largest building, a metal door flung open and a man in an orange parka walked out onto the landing.

Surprise sprang onto his face as he spotted her.

"Whoa!" he said, pulling on his gloves. "Where did you come from?"

Pearly didn't know what to tell him first, so she blurted out everything. "My name is Pearly Woe and my parents have been kidnapped by Emmeline Woods and are locked up in a warehouse on Orchard Island. I need you to call someone to get help, and Ms Woods is out there somewhere with a rifle hunting the Great Hairy Beast and you need to make sure she doesn't find it and shoot it, because ... because that would be terrible. And there's a very sick ... er ... animal around the bend there and if we don't help her soon she may die."

The man's eyes were wide with shock. Then he laughed, and patted her on the back. "Pearly Woe, you say. Well, hello, Pearly. My, you have a lot to say, don't you? But you are a sight for sore eyes. I'm Stefano. Please. Come inside..."

"No!" Pearly shouted and stamped her foot. No one was going to stop her this time. No one. "I am not going inside. You can't make me. I need to get help! You have to help me get help. Please call someone to help my parents—"

"I'm afraid that won't be necessary—"

Pearly couldn't believe what she was hearing. Her whole body trembled. She was a volcano ready to blow its top off. "You have to! That's it. You have to. They need to be rescued... It's that simple! I used to think it was difficult. But it's not. It's simple. I can't

206

fail this time. I might be good at failure but this time I am going to fail at failing – or else! You don't understand..." Pearly plopped onto the step with a thud. She could feel a sob rising up into her throat. She didn't want to cry. She only wanted to get help. Why was it always so hard?

Stefano sat beside her. "No," he said softly, a hint of amusement in his voice. "*You* don't understand. Take a look over there. See that truck that's just pulled in?"

Pearly looked up. Her vision was watery, but she could just make out a large yellow dual cab truck with tractor-like wheels on the other side of the compound. Pearly didn't care about a truck. How was a truck going to help? Two doors opened and a group of four people began to climb out.

"I was coming out to meet them, and–"

Pearly rubbed her eyes and looked again. A tall willowy woman with long red curls streaming out from underneath her beanie and a shorter, stockier man, with a much-missed smile plastered across his face were running towards her and waving wildly. Was it possible? "Is that? Is that..."

"Yes, Pearly. It sure is."

Pearly shot off the step and tore across the ice, stumbling and sliding and twice tumbling right over, but she didn't stop. Not for a second. Not until she was in the arms of Angel and Ricky Woe.

"Pearly!" cried her mother. "We were so worried."

"You're OK," sniffed her father. "We thought we'd lost you for ever."

Pearly drank in their smells, nestled into their warmth. "I'm sorry," she sniffled. "I'm so sorry. I tried. But nothing I did worked."

Her father held her face with both hands. "What are you talking about? Why the apologies? We should be the ones apologizing."

"Absolutely!" said her mother. "We are so, so sorry. We messed up terribly – got sucked in by that Emmeline Woods. She was convincing at first, had us thinking that she was intrigued by the Great Hairy Beast, but all she really wanted was information and Pig. And then when we told her Pig was not for sale and we would not be accompanying her on her trip, well, she turned nasty. Real nasty, real quick. Honey turned to vinegar in a flash. We didn't want to get you involved, but we were desperate and we thought that we had failed you and—"

"You came through," her father interrupted. "You're the reason we're here now."

"But how?" Pearly sobbed. She couldn't stop the tears even if she wanted to. "How? I couldn't get help. That's all you asked and I couldn't find a way. I kept doing everything wrong."

"Oh stop, my love," said her mother, hugging her tight again. "You did everything absolutely right. We're here, aren't we?"

"But I couldn't stop worrying and imagining horrible things. All. The. Time. I couldn't think straight, I worried so much."

Pearly's mother stroked her face. "We all worry, Pearly. It's normal. But to act when you are shaking in your boots and thinking the worst, well, that takes courage, enormous courage. And from what I've heard, that's what you did. You never gave up. You took risks and you took initiative – the most amazing initiative!"

"*Já. Já.* You did," said a familiar voice behind her parents. Pearly turned to see a grinning Felix.

"Felix?" Pearly was both confused and relieved. The giant pulled at his orange beard, grinned a rotten toothy grin and laughed his belly-wobbling laugh. "*Já. Já.* Your message to the police. It got through. They arrived at the ship mere minutes after you left with the Boss Lady."

"We've been looking for you ever since – and when that blizzard came, we thought we'd lost you for sure." Her mother smothered her in yet another hug.

"You are a brave one, Pearly," said Felix. "Sneaking into the common room and getting that message out. That took nerve. I'm sorry I didn't help you more." Felix dropped his fuzzy chin to his chest. "I hate to say it, but I failed you – that woman scared the living daylights out of me."

The tips of Pearly's ears were burning. Her?

Courageous? Had she really been brave?

"Pig!" her father said suddenly. "Oh my, what happened to Pig?" His eyes flashed with fear.

"Pig?" said Stefano.

Pearly had almost forgotten! "He's safe. He's looking after Char on the other side of the mountain."

"Char?" asked her mother, putting her arm across her shoulder and pulling her close as they walked across the compound.

"She's a polar bear and she's very sick. We need to get help quickly. And before Ms Woods finds her with her rifle."

Her parents exchanged worried glances.

"You do realize that there are no polar bears on Antarctica, don't you?" said Stefano. "And no pigs either..." His face was pure disbelief.

"Normally, there aren't," Pearly said with confidence. "But today there are. And the polar bear is very unwell and the pig is looking after her. And Ms Woods is out hunting – with a rifle."

Stefano folded his arms across his chest. "Normally, I would think that you were delirious from the cold, but you are obviously an extraordinary girl, so today – well, today, I am going to say, lead the way!"

EPILOGUE –
THREE DAYS LATER

It was a day of goodbyes.

Some were welcome, Pearly had to admit. It pleased her no end to see the famous Ms Emmeline Woods and her sniffly photographer handcuffed and escorted by two Orchard Island police officers to a waiting aircraft. It looked as though Ms Woods might make headlines after all, but for all the wrong reasons, and that made Pearly smile. The woman deserved it. And Stanley too, even if he wasn't party to Ms Woods's plans – he was well aware that Pearly and Pig were Ms Woods's prisoners, and he did nothing about it.

The best part of the whole affair was how they got caught. It was super exciting to watch Ms Woods and Stanley Snell zoom up to the station on the orange skidoo, requesting help to get back to the *Mighty Muncher*, because their Zodiac had been damaged in the storm. Ms Woods was all fluttering eyelashes and dazzling white teeth until Pearly and her parents appeared. That was a precious moment that Pearly

211

would never forget. Ms Woods denied everything. Said that Pearly's parents must have accidentally locked themselves in that storeroom and that she had no idea how they came to be tied to chairs. It was a pathetic defence, and the police didn't buy it for a second. Nor did they buy Stanley's performance when he broke into a coughing and sneezing fit, collapsed to the ground and announced he had pneumonia and needed to go to hospital, claiming he was also Ms Woods's captive. It too was rather pathetic.

Char was also about to leave. And that was a happy-sad goodbye. Char had been sedated and fed via a drip and then loaded on a research vessel that was heading off to Alaska. She was dopey from the sedatives but she managed to chuff a thank you to Pearly. Pearly hoped that one day she would meet her again – in the Absolutely-Penguin-Free zone of the Arctic Circle.

And now it was time for Pearly and Pig and Ricky and Angel to head home too. The crew on the *Mighty Muncher* had agreed to take them back to Port Clementine, then the ship was off to Iceland. They'd had enough of the Antarctic after the last few weeks.

Pearly longed to say goodbye and to thank Prof. Somehow she had managed to keep from mentioning him or his bunker, and the truth about the Great Hairy Beast, but the secret burned inside her. She reminded herself that being stealthy and respecting the wishes of the people you meet was all part of being a Guild member. And she owed so much to the unusual little man with the fake fur coats and the many secrets. But now they were going. A scientist from the station was taking them in a Zodiac out to the *Mighty Muncher*.

Pearly sat at the front of the boat with her parents and Pig. She looped one arm over Pig's back.

He looked up at her and winked. *You did good, Pearly*, he oinked softly.

"So did you," Pearly replied.

We make a good team.

"I guess we do – the 'smoky bacon' team!"

Pig snorted. He lifted his snout into the air and sniffed in a lungful of the polar air.

Pearly laughed. She was going to miss this vast white continent, despite the anguish it had caused her. She watched as three penguins dived into the sea, and a flock of black sea birds flew overhead in the shape of an arrow, and she listened as her mother talked non-stop about all that had happened. She'd missed her mother's stories.

The scientist sat at the back of the boat, smiling occasionally at Angel's commentary as he navigated the Zodiac expertly through the ice floes, until finally it jutted up against the red hull of the icebreaker. Ricky and Angel worked together to help Pig into the sling that would lift him up. Then they followed him, climbing up the ladder.

Pearly lingered a moment.

The scientist stood, his legs spread apart for balance. He was a short man, clad in the regulation orange snow jacket and trousers that everyone at the station wore. He had his hood tight around his face and a thick scarf wound around his neck and chin to ward against the cold. "Let me be of assistance," he said, holding out his gloved hand.

Pearly froze. She recognized that voice.

The man pulled his scarf from his chin to reveal a thin grey plaited beard.

"How?" said Pearly, astonished.

"You know the answer to that one, Miss Pearly!"

Pearly laughed. "Of course – you have your ways!"

"I knew you were a clever one," he said. He took off his beanie and bowed low. "It has been an honour to meet such a fine Adventurologist, Miss Pearly. *Adieu.*"

Pearly felt blood rush into her face; her arms tingled.

"Not a word," said Prof as he replaced his beanie and helped her onto the ladder.

Pearly nodded and mouthed, *"Merci." Thank you.*

She climbed up into the ship – it was time to head home to Woe Mansion.

She had some serious Adventurologist training to catch up on.

THE
Rules and
Guidelines
for Young
Adventurologists
(THE RAG)

BY GORDON WOE

THE ADVENTUROLOGISTS' GUILD

We are a top-secret group of stealth adventurers founded by Gordon Woe in 1981. We love the thrill of discovery and the challenge of going where no one has gone before. We share a sense of awe and wonder at our blue planet, and are driven to test our limits and to search out unique experiences, but to do so quietly. We take a solemn vow not to draw attention to ourselves, gain profit, record, film or effect change during our adventures. We are not showy TV adventurers. Respect and care of the planet and its people are paramount. Our reward is in meeting the challenge of the adventure itself, of feeling wholly alive, and in satisfying our human curiosity and craving for adrenaline.

The Guild was founded to provide a safe haven for like-minded adventurers, tired of flashy and fake modern-day adventurers and their destructive, self-serving, money-making ways. The Guild offers support and advice to its members, helps to raise funds when needed and trains young would-be Adventurologists.

THE CHARTER:
NO ADVENTURE TOO SMALL.
NO CHALLENGE TOO GREAT.
ADVENTURE BY STEALTH.
LEAVING NO TRACE.

RULES:

RULE 1: Stay alive.

RULE 2: Do not take or destroy.

RULE 3: Tread lightly.

RULE 4: Do not disturb the balance.

RULE 5: Never answer the Adventure Phone – unless an authorized member of the Adventurologists' Guild.

RULE 6: Respect the people you meet and the places you explore.

RULE 7: Never boast, brag, record or publicize your discoveries and adventures. Adventures are to be shared with the Guild only, and on a need-to-know basis.

ADVENTUROLOGING –
THE BASICS

1. Be prepared. Planning is everything.
   Plan. Plan. Plan.
2. Be prepared, but also be prepared to be
   spontaneous, when plans don't go to plan.
3. Know your limits – and plan for this.
4. Push your limits – that's what adventurologing
   is all about.
5. Calculate your risks.
6. Good health and fitness is essential –
   both mind and body. Work hard at it.
7. Follow your passions, as they will guide you to
   the right places.
8. Take the time to savour the wonders you
   uncover – that's also what adventurologing
   is all about.

SURVIVING
STICKY SITUATIONS

1. Take initiative.
2. Think outside the box.
3. Keep your eyes and ears open and your wits about you.
4. Make the impossible possible.
5. Think on your feet.
6. Act quickly and decisively.
7. Don't panic.
8. Logic is your friend.
9. Expect the unexpected.
10. Knowledge is power.

ACKNOWLEDGEMENTS

This story is for the thousands of kids I have met at school visits over the past fifteen plus years. In fact, this story would never have been written if not for the kids who, after listening to my Antarctic adventure story and recovering from the shock of the final reveal, gazed at me with excited eyes and said, *But what happens next?* and *Have you written that story in a book?* Their joyous enthusiasm was my absolute inspiration for creating the characters of Pearly and Pig, putting them on Antarctica and writing this book. So heartfelt thanks to each and every one of you!

Thanks also to the teacher (whose name I can't remember – sorry) who during a school visit long ago regaled me with her Antarctic story, and encouraged me to use the idea behind her story to create my own Antarctic adventure to use in my sessions. I apologize for the memory loss, but regardless, thank her for her generosity and inspiration, and for sparking an idea that I have used for a decade or more to enthuse and enlighten students about story and storytelling.

Thank you to the many clever people who helped me with the various foreign languages Pearly has mastered, but I have not. Thanks especially to: Tess, Lizzie, Simmi, Sibba, Kieran, Sarah, Janine, Jova,

Michelle, Christina, Laure and Meg. Any mistakes are my own.

Many thanks as always to my agent, Pippa Masson, for her feedback, advice and guidance, and to the wonderful sales, marketing and publishing teams at Walker Books Australia. Thanks in particular to my publisher, Linsay Knight, for her continued support and enthusiasm for my stories. Thanks also to designer Sarah Davis and illustrator Rebecca Crane.

And finally thanks to my friends and family for their love and support and for putting up with me during those times when I am lost in a story.

ABOUT THE AUTHOR

Sue Whiting is an award-winning children's and YA author and editor who has worked in publishing for two decades. Sue was senior commissioning editor and publishing manager for Walker Books Australia for many years before leaving in 2016 to concentrate on her writing. As a storyteller and schools' performer, Sue has informed, inspired and entertained thousands of kids across the country. She is also a freelance children's book editor and writing coach, and the author of numerous books, including the bestselling *Missing*, the award-winning *A Swim in the Sea* and a number of CBCA Notable Books. Sue's latest novel *The Book of Chance* was shortlisted for the 2021 CBCA Book of the Year Awards and awarded Highly Commended in the 2021 Davitt Awards.

The
Beatryce
Prophecy

KATE DiCAMILLO
illustrated by **SOPHIE BLACKALL**

*We shall all, in the end, be led to where we belong.
We shall all, in the end, find our way home.*

In a time of war, a mysterious child appears at the
monastery of the Order of the Chronicles of Sorrowing.
Gentle Brother Edik finds the girl, Beatryce, curled in a
stall, wracked with fever, coated in dirt and blood and
holding fast to the ear of Answelica the recalcitrant goat.
As the monk nurses Beatryce to health, he uncovers her
dangerous secret – one that imperils them all.

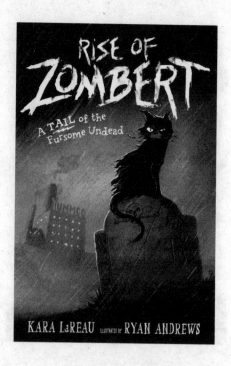

RISE OF ZOMBERT

A TAIL of the Fursome Undead

KARA LaREAU ILLUSTRATED BY RYAN ANDREWS

While helping her best friend Danny film his latest
horror flick, Mellie discovers a scraggly cat behind a
dumpster outside the YummCo Foods factory. Mellie
names the stray Bert and hides him in her room,
knowing her parents won't let her keep him. But soon
Bert has decapitated all her stuffed animals, and before
long he is leaving the headless corpses of birds and
mice as gifts for her. Danny is convinced the cat is a
zombie, living on the brains of its victims. But is that
what's *really* going on?